MOON OF HONEY

LUA DE MEL

TERESA MANIDIS

For Dad, who always told me I could write

Copyright © 2006 Teresa Manidis
Printed in the United States
All rights reserved. No part of this book may be used or reproduced in any manner without written permission. All characters and descriptions are fictional. Any similarity to persons living or dead is purely coincidental.

ISBN: 978-1-84728-158-6

Front Cover: Pousada de Santa Marinha, Guímarães Portugal
Back Cover: Pico's South Coast, Portugal
Both © 2006 Teresa Manidis

Additional copies available at *www.lulu.com* or through your local retailer.

CHAPTER ONE

"*Por favor, leite fresco.*"

The American woman emphasized the last word, *'fresco,'* by opening her eyes wide and nodding vigorously at the waiter, who was staring patiently at the tourist.

"*Sim, Señhora.*"

"*Fresco,*" she repeated, solemnly.

"*Sim, Señhora.* Yes. Fresh milk. No problem."

He sauntered towards the general area of the kitchen.

"Do you think it'll work this time?"

The woman was now addressing the man across the café table, who was engrossed in a back issue of *USA Today*. He was in his late thirties, of medium build, with a thick head of salt-and-pepper brown hair.

"Probably not," he said, good-naturedly. He turned to the sports section.

"But why? How can a whole country have breakfast without milk? Look at these delicious pastries," she glanced down at the decadent collection arranged in front of her. "What are we supposed to drink with them?"

"They do serve canned milk."

"It's not at all the same thing. Back home, evaporated milk is a baking ingredient. I mean, it'd be like – like handing out unsweetened baking chocolate to trick-or-treaters."

She added, self-righteously, "I just prefer regular milk."

"Tourist," her husband teased. And then, to make matters worse he added, smiling, "*American* tourist."

"Oh, I know. I *am* being a tourist. I'm supposed to drink *espresso*," she grimaced, glancing at the tiny white cups scattered all over the outdoor tables. "How can you order that stuff?"

"It's not so bad."

"It tastes just like coffee grounds. Oh well."

And with that last complaint spent, like some strange quota met, the woman inhaled deeply, entwined her fingers and stretched her arms above her head. She glanced around her at the sunny square filled with small, purple flowers, and smiled benevolently. She was in her late twenties; slender, with amber eyes and poker straight, dark brown hair. She turned a now beaming face on her husband and said, "It's a lovely day!"

"It is, darling." Then added, "Feeling better?"

"Much, thank you."

After ten years of marriage, Pete Franklin thought to himself, he knew his wife pretty well. Amelia just loved to fit things into what she considered to be their proper place in her world. She would say, 'This is wonderful,' or 'This is terrible' or 'This is just like something from Hemingway or the Bible or Vogue.' And then there would be no stopping her until she had found satisfactory analogies for everything in her immediate environment. Pete knew there was no real malice in her criticism, nor envy in her admiration. Hers was simply an observant nature, one that liked to draw parallels from her own experience and from the experiences of others (she was an voracious reader). Amelia was, for the most part, delighted with (or at least, interested in) the world around her. And she was, at all times, eager to play (with childlike enthusiasm) that child's game, 'This is the same, this is different.'

"What do you want to do today?" she asked.

"Anything you want, darling," he said, still lazily eyeing his paper. And then, with uncharacteristic swiftness, he threw down the paper, leaned forward and stared passionately into her eyes. "Anything at all, as long as I'm with you."

Amelia smiled despite herself. She still found Pete's

unpredictable oscillation from distraction to devotion amusing.

"Well, I can't very well get away from you. You're carrying the passports," she teased. "Besides, we don't have the kids to take care of, so I guess it's – it's just us."

Just us. The words hung in the air between them.

Amelia looked down, then up. Their eyes met. Pete's look was quite meaningful. Amelia tried not to, then had to smile.

The waiter came with their drinks. He placed the small, porcelain cup in front of Pete. He then presented, with no little flourish, a crystal goblet filled with white liquid, and placed it on the lace tablecloth in front of Amelia.

"*Obrigado* - Thanks," Pete said hastily, his eyes meeting those of the waiter, who smiled his understanding.

No, *Señhor* and *Señhora* do not need anything else. No, they do not want their bill right away – they are in no hurry. They do not wish to be disturbed. They are having that same, eternal conversation that countless men and women had had, at this café and around the world. The waiter, still smiling to himself, turned and left.

Pete, animated anticipation showing on his face, looked back at Amelia.

But it was too late. Her nose was wrinkled up, and she looked exactly like a disgruntled kitten. He looked down at her glass, which was only infinitesimally less full. She said one word:

"Canned."

* * *

"Well, that was a nice day."

The Franklins were back in their *pousada*, the Portuguese answer to the bed and breakfast, minus the breakfast. Faced with ageing fortresses and empty monasteries, the government had decided to convert many of their national monuments into hotels. By adding new (at least by medieval standards) plumbing, electricity and dining facilities, Portugal had experienced a mild economic boost where, previously, only the financial drain of ongoing preservation had been felt.

The Franklins were enjoying their new room immensely. They had, upon arriving in Óbidos, first been ushered into a dark, economy room – with two single beds. Their chambermaid had understood no English, and only a little of what the Franklins considered their best Portuguese. So a trip back down to the concierge had been in order.

"You see, we'd like one bed."

"There are two of you, yes, sir? And the room is clean, yes? Very nice."

"*Sim*, yes, but this is – well, how do you say it, Amelia?"

"I only know how to say 'honeymoon.' I've no idea how to say 'second honeymoon.'"

"Well, give him the honeymoon part, maybe it'll ring a bell." Amelia tried out her most continental smile.

"*Boa tarde, Señhor.* Good afternoon. This is our *lua de*

mel," and then catching the look of surprise on the concierge's face, put up two fingers and added hastily, "*Seguno* – second - *lua de mel*."

And then a torrent of indistinguishable Portuguese. Hugs all around. Ringing for the bellhop. Hearty congratulations.

Still pleasantly confused, and feeling rather lucky, they had then been ushered into what can only be described as a castle tower room. Not because it was made up to look like a Hollywood set, nor because it was part of a Disney theme vacation package. No, the Franklins called it a castle tower room because, quite literally, that is what it was.

The village of Óbidos was completely surrounded by a huge, twenty-five-foot high stone wall, wide enough on top for three men to walk abreast. The wall, made up of massive cut stone, formed an enormous, multi-angled buttress around the town itself, and looked quite like something from a movie. Showing dark and imposing against the sky, and rising much higher than the wall itself, were several large towers. One particular tower (which had once housed desperate knights defending their countrymen) was now called, inexplicably, *Room 203*. Mrs. Franklin had thrown her day's purchases down onto the enormous four-poster bed, and was now peeking out from one of the openings in the wall.

"It must have been awfully hard to shoot arrows from here. I mean, the slit's so thin, you can only shoot straight in front of you."

"At least, it would be hard to be *hit* by an arrow, if you were in here."

"I guess so."

Amelia was investigating her surroundings. She was on the second level of their suite. A wooden half-ladder/half-stair had led them up to their bedroom, which consisted solely of the afore-mentioned bed (festooned with red velvet drapery and covers) and an emblazoned coat-of-arms above it. The lower level held an (again, red velvet) couch; what can only be described as an empty (Amelia had peeked) pirate's chest; an end table; telephone; and the requisite trap door.

"What do you think's down there?" asked Amelia, motioning towards the floor.

"Skeletons, most likely."

"Do you think it's locked?"

"Check."

Amelia, with the seriousness only a child (or the child-like) can muster at such times, solemnly lifted the ancient wrought-iron ring. She gasped as the door creaked open, revealing chalky stone steps leading down into inky blackness.

"What do you see?" Pete asked.

"Nothing. Absolutely *nothing*. Oh, it's so mysterious. Like something from a book. I'm terrified, *deliciously* terrified. I don't want to go down there – the stairs are five hundred years old if they're a day – but, if I don't, I'll never forgive myself!"

"You know, you are so sexy right now."

"Stop your nonsense, Pete, I'm serious."

"So am I."

"Peter!"

To her dying day, Amelia would wonder what lay beneath the trap door in Óbidos.

* * *

"Where shall we eat tonight?"

Pete was taking his wife's carry-on luggage down from the over-head rack, in preparation to disembark. The small *Crusiero de Canal* was slowly churning into the principal port of Horta, on the island of Fíal.

"We haven't even gotten off the ferry yet, Pete!"

"I know, but the *food* on these islands! Don't you remember?"

Yes, Amelia thought, she remembered the Azore Islands well.

Ten years ago, as a college Senior pouring through atlases in the reference section of the library, Amelia had first spotted the Azores. Not as the gorgeous, green, hydrangea-laden mountains climbing out of a lapis sea that she was to soon fall in love with, but as tiny white dots on a baby blue grid, about an inch and a half to the left of mainland Portugal.

The islands had, at the time, represented *compromise*. Pete was enamored of the rustic-European-village idea of a honeymoon, while Amelia was firm in her desire to 'go to the islands.' All their other wedding plans had been finalized; this was the last major decision. And then, the Azores had appeared on the horizon – European islands, islands they had never even known to exist; mysterious islands, fabled to be all that was still visible of the Lost Continent of Atlantis.

The newly wed Franklins had not been disappointed in their decision to have a Portuguese *lua de mel*. They had thoroughly enjoyed their week spent on the mainland, traveling north from Lisbon through Sintra, Fátima and Guímarães. The *pousadas* they had stayed at were majestic; the massive historic monuments they had visited, impressive. But it was the islands, these unpretentious, humble islands that they were to remember with the most affection; it was on these islands that they truly had honeymooned; and it was to these islands that they were now, so eagerly returning.

Besides, the food was incredible.

"How about Alfredo's?" Superb service. Enormous, whole, deep-fried fishes, eyes still in. Irresistible local blueberry liqueur. And then, the award-winning (and Alfredo himself would insist upon showing you the gold plaque) passion fruit pudding for dessert.

"Good, but how about Pedro's?" What would be a five star restaurant in the states, for about ten bucks a person. Raw fillet mignon placed on a hot lava rock on your own plate. Seared to perfection. Eaten when you could no longer wait another second.

"Ah, that's good stuff. But," something was holding Pete

back. As he gave his luggage ticket to the taxi driver, he felt the pangs of indecision. As good as these restaurants had been, something inside was nagging him, making him more and more certain that he had forgotten something.

The taxi now rumbled over narrow but empty cobblestone streets. Here there would be no postcard stands to avoid, no crowded souvenir shops spilling out onto the street like in London or Paris or Rome.

For Fíal, like her eight sister islands, had never been a great tourist attraction. Isolated both geographically and culturally from the rest of the world, her breath-taking natural beauty and wild, black sandy beaches were simply too remote for the average traveler to access. The only people who came here now were sailors. Not the great Portuguese explorers who once came to top-off their holds (one could almost imagine a sign reading, 'Last stop before New World'). No, not they, but the modern-day rich now sailed into port. Yachts and sailboats arrived daily in the summer months, making either the first or the last stop on a much more comfortable voyage than Columbus ever took.

The Franklins were pulling into the flag-stoned courtyard of their private villa. Masses of scarlet blossoms hung from the white marble veranda. An ancient fountain still sputtered in the yard.

When they had first come to Fial, the newly-weds had stayed at the institutional 'state hotel.' Unlike the *pousadas* of the mainland, this hotel (although still government-run) had been built along totally utilitarian lines and was consequently hideous. This time, and for about the same dollar amount, the Franklins had secured 'a private residence, complete with maid service, laundry and cook (optional).' They were glad of the 'cook (optional)' clause; with all their favorite restaurants to re-visit, it seemed unlikely they would need one.

They explored the ancient and enormous house, while a dog's far-away barking, and the nearby droning of the bees in the blossoms added to the drowsy and dream-like quality of the whole scene.

Suddenly, Pete yelled. Amelia started.

"What now?"

"I've got it! *O Birraca!*"

That was the name of the place that had escaped him. A tiny, low-ceilinged dining room, constructed of dark, rough-hewn logs. Miniscule glazed windows giving onto a side street, admitting the smallest modicum of light. A few local sailors drinking in one corner. And then, the calamari.

The last time Pete had set foot in Fial, he had been experiencing the mad joy and triumph of first love. Having successfully carried off to a remote locale the first girl he had ever kissed, the days and nights (especially the nights) of his three-week tour blurred together in an agreeable haze. Every once in a while, a particular place or taste or sensation would stand out from the rest, or be associated with an even greater pleasure.

And the calamari was one of those things that stood out.

Whether or not the exotic food had augmented Pete's virility and strength, the Franklins had gone back and ordered the same dish (from the same astonished waiter) two nights in a row.

"O Birraca," Pete repeated, smiling assuredly.

"Oh, boy," Amelia laughed, rolling her eyes.

CHAPTER TWO

OBirraca, like most of Fíal, had not visibly changed much in a decade. Its interior had been stained a darker shade of brown, and two of the nine china plates depicting the islands had fallen off the wall, with predictable results. The owner of the establishment had seen fit to fill in the two gaps with a small, brass crucifix and an advertisement for loose-leaf tobacco.

The Franklins were lingering over their port, yet another local specialty.

"Another nine days and we'll be home," said Amelia.

"Yes," Pete sighed, "Back to the old grindstone."

Neither Pete, in his position as senior environmental engineer, nor Amelia as part-time college professor, and mom, was unhappy in their life's work. They were simply indulging in that melancholy conversation all contented tourists enjoy when they still have a good week's vacation ahead of them.

"It's been a wonderful get-away so far."

"Hmm," agreed Pete.

And then, disconnectedly, Amelia asked, "You don't remember where the ladies' room is in this place, do you?"

"I don't think I patronized the *ladies'* room last time I was here."

"You know what I mean."

"I don't see one. Downstairs, maybe? Or back by the kitchen?"

"I'll ask. Do you have the travelers' cheques?"

"Yep. I'll settle up then," said Pete, picking up a pen.

As Pete got down to figuring out the intricacies of gratuity in a foreign country, Amelia took her handbag and approached the waiter who was clearing off the sideboard. The Franklins had been the last patrons of the evening.

"*Por favor, ónde esta el cuarto de Señhoras?*"

"*Sim,*" he replied earnestly. "Through here," he said in halting English, opening a door. "Down steps. Turn left."

And then he obligingly pantomimed, first 'going down steps;' and then, jerkily turning his body to the side, 'turning left.'

"*Obrigada,*" she thanked him.

The waiter flicked on the lone bulb which lighted the

anorexic steps. They alternately creaked or popped loudly in protest as she descended them. The dim light faintly illuminated the faded print of a smiling Madonna at the foot of the stairs.

From where Amelia now stood, a narrow, low-ceilinged hall ran from right to left. The stone floor, painted white and glistening with moisture, showed in two, thin strips on either side of the ruined oriental runner. The air around her was close and damp. To the right, the hallway ended abruptly in a tangle of machinery, choking on its own twisted pipes. This area also housed the only other light source (another low-wattage bulb), as well as a door, leading presumably to the *cuarto de Señhores* – men's room.

Amelia moved in the opposite direction, peering down what was a much longer passageway. The hallway here was in semi-darkness due to a darkened bulb above her head.

"How annoying."

She tried the handle of the first door she reached, but it was locked. "Store room," she considered silently.

Further ahead, she heard water dripping and thought she saw the glimmer of glass. "Wine cellar," she checked-off mentally.

Before reaching it, however, she discovered a second door. She pushed hard, and the heavy door resisted at first and then opened, revealing complete darkness beyond.

"They're certainly thrifty with the electric," she thought to herself.

Halfway in the doorway, she groped around inside for a light-switch and found one. Amelia walked in, then stopped short.

Standing a few feet in front of her was a man, filthy and panting for breath. He had dropped down from the overhead window, which he had just re-closed. Now he stood glaring at Amelia.

If Amelia were the Amelia of ten years previous; a silly, romantic, easily frightened girl; enamored of mystery thrillers and late night television, she would have screamed the house down without thinking twice. Here she was, alone, in a back-alley cellar with a disheveled criminal, who was guilty of (at least) forced entry, and who knew how much worse.

But for some reason she paused before calling out. Perhaps it was because she was no longer a girl. She was older now, a mother. She had seen sickness; sadness; even terror in the eyes of a feverish child. She had learned a little of life. She had been forced, almost against her will, to mature; to recognize pain; to cultivate a sense of empathy.

Or maybe it was just something in his eyes. His incredibly desperate eyes.

The strange man took advantage of her hesitation to step slightly forward, and begin, in grade-school Spanish,

"*Por favor, señorita. Por favor, ayudate, ayudate.*"

Amelia looked him over. He was about 23, 24. He had a

muscular, agile build. His accent had betrayed him as an American. His clothes, upon a closer look, were good quality; it was only the mud and other stains that had made them look in tatters. His curling, blond hair was tousled and strewn with cobwebs, but his face was clean-shaven. The more she looked at him, the more she *felt* (for the lightening-fast feelings known as intuition were at work here, not reason) that here was a man, not so much malevolent as (again, that word) *desperate.*

Amelia made up her mind.

In a calm, clear voice (which even surprised herself), she said, "I believe you meant to say, '*Por favor, Señhora, por favor ajudame, ajudame,*' not, '*ayudate.*'"

Then seeing his blank look, she translated,

"'Please, lady, please help *me*, help *me*' not 'help *you.*' *I* am perfectly alright."

The man just stared, his mouth falling slightly open. He was unable to speak for several seconds.

"You're – you're *American.*"

Amelia's eyebrows went up in assent.

"Here, of all places in the world, I run into - *you.*"

The stranger, simultaneously shaking his head and running his fingers through his hair (dislodging some but not all of the cobwebs) smiled for a second in disbelief. Then all of his former darkness and desperation returned.

"Listen, please," he began. "I don't know how, or why –

you've got absolutely no reason to believe me, or even listen, but please..."

"I'm listening."

At that moment, the man jerked his head over his shoulder towards the grimy, etched window. Amelia thought she heard voices outside, and vague shadows sped past.

"There's no time now," he cried, agony in his voice. "They've followed me here. It's the police!"

"Are you a criminal, then?" Amelia asked softly.

"No. Yes. No, not the way you mean. Please, they'll be down here in a second. What is this place? Can I get out?"

His eyes, tragic and beautiful; once blue but now bloodshot, raced around the room like some cornered, wild animal's. But the man could see plainly that there was nowhere to hide.

A sink, a chair and a lone commode (without even a stall) comprised the tiny room.

Now Amelia heard muffled voices upstairs. She spoke quickly.

"You are in a restaurant. There is only a wine cellar and a locked storeroom, I think, down here; besides the bathrooms, of course. There is one stair leading up to the dining room, that's all."

Their eyes met.

Upstairs, Amelia could hear the waiter's voice raised in anger. The man looked again at the window, which was now almost completely taken up with amorphous shadows. He covered his mouth with his hand, slid it down over his chin, and worked it; anxiously rubbing and re-rubbing where his stubble would have been.

Then, stiffly, he sat down on the hard wooden chair, slowly joined his hands in front of him, and, staring at the crumbling floor, spoke in a low, defeated voice.

"You had better go. It is not safe. They are not coming to arrest me; they are coming *to kill me.*"

The rickety basement stairs thundered under the weight of heavy feet.

The stranger looked up at Amelia, the shadow of a smile playing around his piteous mouth.

"I'm glad to have met you, here at the end. To have seen just one, decent American before I died." He hung his head. "Go."

They were in the passage now. Above the booming Portuguese shouts, she could just make out Pete's tenor voice calling out to her.

"'Melia! 'Melia! Where are you?"

With one swift motion, Amelia stepped towards the door and slammed the bolt shut.

In an instant, the man was on his feet; eyes shining, nostrils flared, face alert. Every muscle in his conditioned body was taught, responsive, ready to spring. He might still be trapped, but his despondency had gone. His will to live emanated from his every pore.

"He's so young," Amelia thought benevolently. Young and beautiful.

Then, surprised, "*I'm* still young. I would hate to die now if I were him. Life is too . . ."

Her split-second reverie was shattered by the pounding on the door. The man ducked down, stalking backwards and away from the door till his outstretched hands touched the far wall. He crouched down, beneath and to the left of the window. His gaze fastened on Amelia.

"*Aberto! Aberto la porta! Isto es las policias!*"

"At once! Open! At this moment!"

"'Melia!"

Dust and a little plaster dislodged from the doorframe as the pounding continued. Amelia's brow was drawn, her bottom lip caught in her teeth. Then, incongruously, her face suddenly brightened. She smirked.

Turning towards the door, she demanded (in a voice not her own), "What the hell is going on?" Then, "Stop it!" as the door seemed about to give way.

"*Señhora, isto es las policias! Aberto la porta!*"

"I most certainly will not open the door! Go away!"

"*Señhora, aberto . . ,*" interrupted by another voice, "I am the Inspector de Sousa. I speak the English. I . . ."

"Go away," Amelia cried again, but now her voice was weak, cracking.

"Is sorry to inconvenience to you. Is most sorry. . ."

"Oh, I'm so sick. What did I eat?" Her voice was gravelly.

"Peter," she called out. "Peter, are you there? Oh . . .

"Amelia! What's happened? I'm here!"

"Peter, make them go away. They're crazy. Why are they – oh, my stomach!" she moaned loudly. She was panting shallowly now.

"*Señhora*, we look for a man . . ."

"Go away, I . . ."

Amelia, clutching her stomach and stumbling audibly towards the sink, filled the discolored enamel cup that stood near the faucet. She swayed and, to the spellbound stranger, she actually seemed about to faint. She then proceeded to make such a cacophony of esophageal sounds as would have made her third grader's classmates proud. She crowned her performance by dashing the cup's contents squarely onto the stone floor.

"Oh, *Señhora*, I apologize."

"Please," came Peter's trembling voice, "My wife is very ill and you're upsetting her. Amelia, let me in!"

"No," came the shaky reply, after a moment's pause. "No. The worst – is over. Give me some space, all of you. For pity's sake," she added, petulantly.

"But, darling, I'll help you!"

"If you want to help me," the words came laboriously, in between deep gulps of air, "Go back and - get me a change of clothes."

"*Señhora*, we apologize. We are much troubled. But we look for a man, a criminal man. He goes this way. We think he goes in restaurant. We need find him, need look in every room."

Looking directly at the man against the wall, she demanded in a slightly stronger voice,

"Don't you think I'd notice it if there were a man in here with me?"

Her voice continued to gain strength as she continued.

"There is nothing in here but a sink – a chair – a filthy toilet – and, and,"

Her voice rose in excitement.

"Oh, no. Oh, *no!*. Peter! Peter, help!"

"What is it?"

"*Que es?*"

"Is it the man? The criminal man?"

In a hoarse, gasping whisper came the answer.

"It's – it's a mouse! Peter, there's a mouse in here! I'm *terrified* of mice!"

And then, after smiling smugly at the stranger, she screamed for 30 seconds straight.

* * *

Having apparently wasted enough time with the insane American, the police left O Birraca, after a brief and unsuccessful search of the rest of the premises. A solitary officer was left behind to patrol the street out front.

Pete, upset by the evening's excitement, and dumbfounded by his wife's sudden illness (as well as her sudden fear of mice), set off for a replacement outfit. "Don't forget *underwear*," she had called out as a parting shot for de Sousa, certain that the Inspector had still been able to hear her.

Now, in the relative calm that ensued, she felt only *slightly* guilty about leaving Pete in the dark. She really hadn't dared to tell him everything while she had been uncertain if *all* of the policemen had left the building. Anyway, she had had a hard enough time convincing him to actually go back to the villa without her. And then there had been the owner to consider; as well as the waiters; kitchen staff and even the neighbors who *might* have overheard her. No, she would talk to him about it.

Later.

She now walked away from the door, through which she had just said goodbye to Pete, and turned towards the man behind her.

He was regarding her with a look of amazement. He grinned - a boyish, rakish smile - and silently pantomimed applause. Amelia bowed with a flourish. She looked up at the window. Light from the street-lamp defused through the yellowing glass, unencumbered now by any shadows. As far as she could make out, the coast was clear. She must work fast. She snatched up her purse, which had landed in a corner. She pulled out what cash she had with her, and stuffed it into the man's hands. He closed his hands around it, keeping her hands tightly in his and pulling her towards him, as she had been about to move away.

"Why?" He mouthed the words silently, searching in her eyes for the answer.

Amelia smiled, squeezed his hands then let go.

She pulled the chair over to the wall, stood on it and reached for the window.

"Ready?" she asked silently.

Raising both palms upwards, as if to say 'you're the boss,' he waited.

Amelia tilted the window upwards, locking it into place above her head.

She looked out.

The street was quiet. A light drizzle was falling on the cobblestones, which glowed yellow in the streetlight. To her immediate left was the entrance to O Birraca. The police officer stood on its steps, turning up his collar to the rain. He now looked inquisitively at Amelia.

"*Señhora?*"

"I needed the air," she said, dramatically fanning her hands towards her face and taking deep breaths.

"*Sim, compreendo.*"

She hung her head in her hands, smiling mischievously as her face was covered. Having successfully dispensed with

Fíal's entire police force, she was now displaying a marked lack of respect for this last representative of law and order.

"My husband – uh - *mi marido?*" she inquired vaguely.

"*A casa. Ele returno a casa, Señhora.*"

"Ah*, sim.* He went back to the house, of course. Oh, *meu stômago.*"

Then, "*Por favor, Señhor, es possivel* – is it possible to obtain – *a obter una Coca-cola?*" She motioned weakly towards the restaurant. Muffled sounds came from inside; the clink of plates.

"*Por favor,*" she pleaded.

"*Sim, Señhora.*" The rain had increased, and the policeman was eager to get inside under any pretext. He turned and entered the restaurant.

"Quick!" Amelia whispered.

The man was beside her in an instant. She cupped her hands, ready to help him up.

He hesitated.

"Hurry. He'll be out in a second."

He still looked down at her, searchingly.

"Please," she begged, "What is it they say? You save somebody's life, and then you feel responsible for him for the rest of your own. Look. If you need anything, my husband and I are on the Rue Verde, 61, the white villa. You can't miss it. Now go."

She held out her cupped hands. He grabbed the window

ledge above him, but otherwise remained still, gazing at her.

"I know I've got no right to ask for anything else," he began, his voice venturing above a whisper. "Besides, it could put you and your husband in danger."

Amelia remained silent, looking steadily into his eyes. He shifted his weight, then continued.

"But if I gave you something, could you try and get it back to the US with you? It's got to get to the State Department."

He slipped a thin, silvery strip into her already outstretched hand. Glancing down for a split second, Amelia thought it looked rather like a gum wrapper. Amelia closed her fingers around it.

"Thanks, again," he said, exhaling deeply and inclining his head down towards hers; "You really are amazing."

Muted voices, laughter came from above. Outside, the misty rain billowed in great, golden sheets.

Time stood still.

Amelia asked, slowly, "What are you wanted for?"

The fugitive leaned over, kissed her fully on the mouth, and said one word.

"Murder."

He pulled himself up and out the window, unassisted, and ran off into the night. A moment later, the policeman came out with a soda and handed it to Amelia through the still open window.

"*Muito obrigado*," she murmured.

CHAPTER THREE

T he taxi pulled away from 61 Rue Verde. Pete Franklin was supporting his wife's arm, as they tentatively ascended the grand staircase. Amelia was hunched over, and lifted her head only enough to steal a sideways glance out of the enormous windows that gave onto the drive. Once the red taillights were no longer in view, she straightened up, dug her fingers into Pete's arm, and yanked him up the stairs behind her.

"Come on!" she called wildly.

Pete was too stunned to follow right away, so she had gained the bedroom and flung herself down on the settee by the time he entered the room. She was on her back, kicking her heels in the air like a gleeful schoolgirl. She was actually squealing (there is no other word for it), and her face glowed with excitement.

"I'm *dying* to tell you all about it!" she began at once.

"Tell me - all about it?" Pete could only repeat her words lamely.

"Yes," she began at break-neck speed. "I couldn't let on in the car because this town's so small I thought the taxi driver might talk if I looked *too* vigorous. I had to put on a good act, you know, having to be *helped* up the stairs and all that nonsense. I hope it worked. He didn't seem *too* curious. And then all that fuss with de Sousa; you've no *idea* how clever I've been! Why, you don't even know about the Coca-Cola trick yet!"

Pete stood stock-still, staring at his wife.

"Why, Pete. What's wrong? You look so funny. Well, I guess I *do* have some explaining to do," she admitted, sheepishly. "Let's see, oh yes. Well, I went down to find the bathroom and then . . . "

Amelia recapitulated, with great gusto, the greater part of the evening's events.

"And so, by the time the policeman came out with the soda, the man was gone!" she finished triumphantly.

Pete didn't speak. He wore an expression his wife couldn't quite place, and she found that fact, in and of itself, strangely disquieting.

"Well," she demanded at last, still trying to be jubilant, but a little annoyed that Pete hadn't been more appreciative of her story. "What do you think? Can you believe it?"

Pete sat down on the edge of the bed. When he spoke at last, his voice was very low.

"I *think* I understand what you've been trying to tell me," Pete mirrored. "You were never sick."

"No."

"You were just play-acting?"

"No. Well, kind of. Yes, I guess you could say that."

"Alright."

Pete looked pale when he spoke again.

"Let me see if I got this straight. You found a criminal in the basement, and instead of calling out for help, you harbored him, lied to the police (and to me), gave him your money and then helped this same man escape by even more deception on your part."

"Peter, if you're going to put it like that! You make me seem ridiculous. No, you haven't gotten it at *all* right. I mean, maybe the facts are like that, but really! Harboring criminals, deceiving police – you make it sound like we're in court!"

"And we might just end up there! Don't you see the seriousness of the situation?"

Amelia laughed. "And don't you see the fun? The

excitement?" Her eyes glowed. " I can't remember when I've had a better time!"

She stretched out on the settee, smiling coyly, her eyes inviting Pete to join her.

He didn't move. Amelia sat up, frowning.

With a rapidity possible only between those who have been intimate, the mood suddenly cooled and the conversation took on a different tone.

"Lighten up, Pete, for heaven's sake. And give me a little credit. I think (and *I'll* say it since you're not going to) that I've been very clever. I mean, what else could I have done, given the situation? Remember, there wasn't a lot of time to think."

"No, thinking hasn't been your strong point tonight," Pete said coldly.

Amelia visibly stiffened.

"The only sensible thing you could have done," he continued flatly, "Was to call for help when you discovered this guy down there. Or at least run up and get me. Why didn't you? You know, you've left me completely out of everything tonight, completely. You – you've played me for a fool."

"Don't be ridiculous, I've already told you,"

But Pete interrupted with, "Was he handsome?"

"What? Tch!" Amelia sputtered in disgust, averting her eyes.

"You're acting like an absolute child. That has nothing to do with this."

"Was he?"

Had Amelia been looking in his eyes, she might have seen the warning in them.

"Pete, you are being absurd. You've taken everything I said in completely the wrong way. I did what I could, given the situation. I'm sorry if you don't agree, or think I was being foolish, or if you feel 'left out.' Really, I thought you would find it all funny. Let's forget all about it. Come on. . ."

"Was he?" Pete yelled fiercely.

Peter Franklin had yelled at his wife exactly twice in his life. Once was when they were newly married, with a baby on the way, and had been arguing about whose family to go to for Christmas. The second time was nine years later in a villa in Fíal.

Amelia felt her thighs begin to shake. Then her stomach, for the first time that night, began to tighten and quiver.

'I won't be sick, I won't!"

She tried to *will* her body to calm itself, but ten years of relative security had not conditioned her for this. Her body was viscerally responding, even before her mind could focus. All she could see was a kind of colored haze, a swirling vacuum into which her happiness was vanishing for, apparently, no reason at all.

And standing in the middle of that haze was a stranger she did not recognize.

"I will not cry in front of him," her pride raged inside her, "I will not give him that satisfaction."

Standing up to her full height, and just before slamming the bathroom door behind her, she whipped out at him,

"Much more handsome than you!"

* * *

Pete looked at himself in the mirror, under the unforgiving fluorescent lights.

He had cleared out with his pillow after Amelia had slammed the master bathroom door, and was now in the tiny powder room on the floor below. He was naked from the waist up, having just splashed cold water over his face and neck.

He regarded himself again.

Come on, what the hell had happened up there? He'd lost it, completely lost it. What had he been raging about? Had he been yelling, actually yelling at Amelia?

He remembered demanding, demanding . . . *what*, exactly? He had been asking if the man his wife had helped had been handsome. A simple question, really.

But if it had been so simple, why hadn't Amelia just answered it right away? Why hadn't she been able to look at him? Why had he started to see red even before the words were out of his mouth? What was nagging him?

What was the question he had really wanted to ask her?

Pete looked at the man in the mirror. His eyes looked puffy at this hour and a little red. Forty this Christmas, he thought.

Graying around the edges. A little soft around the middle – alright, a little more than a *little* soft around the middle.

What was happening to him? Was he getting old? Or was he getting *jealous*? Of what?

Amelia, as she said, had just been having a little fun. She had always loved excitement and adventure, placating herself with paperback novels and local theatre productions. Now, she had finally had (and thoroughly enjoyed) a taste of the real thing. Why should he grudge her that so much? What did he think this stranger, a man she'd never even met before, could possibly mean to his wife?

'Nothing, of course. Get a handle on yourself. You're just imagining things.'

But why get so upset tonight? Pete had never been the jealous type before; he had never needed to be with Amelia.

What did that mean? That he had never needed to be jealous where his own wife was concerned? Why not?

Was she unattractive? Certainly not that. Amelia had always been pretty, damned pretty in fact. That's one of the reasons he had fallen in love with her. He loved her eyes, her hair, her athletic build; she had been a runner all her life, even through her pregnancies.

'She has the same body she had in college,' he thought, ruefully looking at his own reflection. Then, somewhat surprised, 'No. She has a better *body* now than she did then.'

Well, all right, she was pretty. Good looking. Even

attractive, *to him*. But to *other* men? Why was that idea so foreign from his thinking of Amelia?

'She's not the type,' he argued with himself. 'She's - she's sweet. And wholesome. Everybody *likes* her. Lots of men *like* her, they just don't fall in love with her. She's more like everybody's kid sister. Or the girl next door. She's – she's just . . . *Amelia.*'

Why did Pete have the sinking feeling that he was losing this argument against himself? He started reaching for straws;

'She's a mom' – but, unfortunately, that couldn't automatically disqualify her. 'She's getting older' – but just shy of 30 seemed uncomfortably young at the moment.

'She's, she's' –

But whatever objections he offered, in the end, he was faced with the fact that he was married to someone who was young; attractive; and attractive possibly not only to himself.

'But she's *mine!*' his ego cried out, desperately. '*Mine*, and always has been. *Mine*, and always will be.'

But tonight, for the first time, his sub-conscious had felt some intangible danger to the *status quo*. Some sense of his had been heightened; some warning light inside him had been switched on for the first time.

Had he been taking his wife for granted? He had assumed that he would always be able to provide Amelia with all she could want in a man. Could she desire *more* out of life?

'She is mine, she is content!' His fear called out, blindly, wildly. 'She is not attractive to other men and she is not attracted by them. *I am enough for her, always.*'

And then, staring at the man in the mirror, Pete Franklin found the question he had been trying to ask all along.

'Am I enough?'

'Will I always be enough?'

'Is our life together enough?'

'Will she always care?'

'Am I enough?'

And not knowing the answer to this question, the once-raging man, now quiet in his desperation and pain, turned off the light.

*　*　*

The sun rose over the orchard, spilling into the courtyard and dancing on the white, muslin curtains in Amelia's room. By the time the first rays had crept onto her pillow, she was already half awake.

She had had a restless night, full of anxious dreams. Her head ached, and for a moment she wondered if she had been drinking the night before. Then she remembered.

Amelia got up and padded softly over to the windows. She pulled the curtains back and looked out. All yellow and gold and crimson and azure.

Funny, she thought, how a day can be so mercilessly beautiful. But then, the weather never cared much about being suitable to the occasion. She could think of any number of weddings besieged by relentless rain; and just as many funerals on bright, sunny days.

She got dressed.

The getting dressed and noting the weather part had taken all of seven minutes. Now, she stood halfway to the door, undecided if she wanted to meet Pete yet, but quite sure she couldn't cloister herself in her suite all day.

"Well, I have no choice," she said aloud, taking a step forward.

At that moment, the door opened and Pete walked in.

The first thing she noted was that he seemed dressed for church; tie, jacket and all. He had nicked himself shaving, and looked more like an uncomfortable parochial school boy than anything else. He swallowed, hard, then spoke.

"Amelia," he voice was hoarse, "Am I enough?"

"You're an idiot."

"I know that," he acceded quickly, "But *am I enough*?" He looked miserable.

"Enough of an idiot?"

"No, just enough for you."

"You're talking nonsense."

"I know it sounds like nonsense but it's – it's very important to me that I know the answer. You see, I know I got crazy last night but that's because I didn't know what else to do. I felt, somehow, that – that I was *losing* you."

"Losing me to what? You're still not making sense."

"Just losing you, that's all," he stumbled on, exasperated. "I mean, I always thought you'd be there for me, when the kids grew up, when we got old . . . Then, last night, there was something in your eyes that I'd never seen before. You were so elated, so excited it scared me. I thought, 'My God, I'm losing her. I can't make her that happy. She'll need it, and leave me to go after it."

"Go after what?"

"Everything I'm not. Danger, excitement, adventure, romance – just everything!"

"I see." Amelia looked thoughtful. After a moment, she went on.

"You were scared last night of something you thought you saw inside me?"

"Yes."

"You thought you were losing me to – to a stranger?

"Well, not so much to *him* as to – well, just all he represents."

"Which is . . ?"

"I've already told you. Passion, excitement, everything."
She paused again.

"What do you think you are to me?" she asked evenly.

"That's – that's what I don't know anymore. I thought I was enough, but maybe I was taking things for granted. You've got to tell me, Amelia, either way. I love you more than I loved you the day we got married. Even if things go all wrong," his voice cracked, "I think I'll always love you, with all my heart. But – but you must let me know."

Amelia looked unsure, as if still appraising the situation. Then, finally, with a little nod she said simply, "You're enough."

Pete sighed in relief.

"But," she added, "You're still an idiot."

* * *

Since the weather was so enticing, the Franklins decided to eat *al fresco*. Amelia resigned herself to drinking orange juice, having given up completely in her elusive search for milk. Pete, only too eager to be helpful, had made enough *omellete* for ten. Unseasonably cool for August, the crisp breeze from the coast was the perfect complement to the deeply penetrating sun.

They had been largely silent throughout their meal. They now regarded each other from across the table.

"If I promise not to bite your head off, would you tell me a little more about last night?"

"No, thank you! 'Fool me once, shame on you' and all that."

"No, please. I'm interested."

"In what?"

"Why."

"'Why' what?"

"Why you did those incredible things you did - took those risks, for a complete stranger."

Amelia looked suspiciously at her husband, searching his eyes for something she did not find. Then she replied.

"Intuition."

"Go on," Pete coaxed, gently. *Please, God, if only I can get her to talk.*

Amelia put down her fork.

"Well, a lot of people think intuition's silly. Kind of the opposite of reason, or intellect. But intuition is really one of the best tools we have already 'built-in,' so to speak."

Pete looked interested with all his might.

"A new person walks into the room. Immediately, and without any conscious effort on your part, you start making a million observations about him. Most are pretty simple – 'I know this person,' 'He's a stranger,' 'I feel threatened,' 'I feel safe' - but just because these observations are *simple*, that doesn't mean they're unimportant."

She went on.

"Police all over the world use their intuition everyday; although, to be politically correct, they have to call it by different names. They use it at security checkpoints in airports; in banks; at press conferences with the president. A computer or metal detector can never replace intuition for picking up subtleties of speech or inflection or eye contact."

"So you're saying everyone has intuition, or just some people?"

"Oh, everyone *has* it. It's just that most people ignore it, or

39

try to rationalize it away. For example, say I was hailing a taxi at the airport, late at night. The car door opens, and the driver gets out to help me with my luggage. He doesn't say or do anything suspicious. But for some, unexplained reason (but I explain it by intuition), the hair on the back of my neck goes up, I can feel my heart race and my adrenalin surge. I'm experiencing the 'flight or fight' response; my big cue that I'm in danger. What do I do? Tell him I've changed my mind, and wait for another taxi? Or chide myself that 'I'm being silly,' or 'over-reacting,' or 'will hurt his feelings' if I don't' get into the back seat of sound-proof vehicle that I will have no control over?"

"I see. And that's how it was last night?"

"No, that's *how it wasn't last night*. When I walked into that room, I waited for the fraction of a second it takes for my intuition to kick in; to tell me to run or scream; to tell me I was in terrible danger. But nothing happened. Nothing on the radar; not a blip. Then he told me something of himself; and again, no red flags went up. I know it must seem crazy to someone who wasn't in that room; to ignore all the facts – breaking and entering, the police hunt, all that. But I *was* in that room, and I know what I felt. I just had to help him. I knew he wasn't dangerous or vicious; in fact, I'm having a hard time picturing him as *any* kind of criminal, even a white collar one. I mean, that's how non-threatening he rated on my intuition scale. I could be totally wrong, but I'd be really surprised."

Pete picked his words carefully.

"Well, thank you for talking to me about it, and I'm sorry we ever argued over it in the first place. I can see your perspective now, and given what you say about intuition, it makes some sense; although I still wish you had involved me. I guess one of the reasons I was so angry last night was really because I was so scared something might have happened to you, alone with a man wanted by the police. I don't care how nice he looked, I don't want anything happening to *you*."

He bit his lower lip, sighed, then continued with characteristic optimism, "Well, we were having a wonderful vacation before all this happened, and I'm sure we can go right back to it. Let's put it all behind us. It's a beautiful day and we've still got plenty of time to ourselves; to explore or relax or do anything we want."

Amelia smiled.

"Besides," he added assuredly, "I'm sure we'll never see this man again."

Pete Franklin had never been so wrong in his life.

CHAPTER FOUR

The Franklins were just getting ready to go into town, when one of the maids came into the sitting room and handed them an official looking card.

"*Señhor* de Sousa," she said in explanation.

"That Inspector person?" Pete looked at his wife, anxiety showing on his face.

She in turn wore a hard, calculating look.

"Send him in," Amelia said calmly, then remembering the language barrier added, "*Sim, sim. Es* 'okay.'"

The maid left the room.

Pete grabbed Amelia's arm.

"What are we going to say?" he whispered, hoarsely.

"Leave it to me."

He found her level-headedness unbearable. "But, maybe he's found out something!"

"I don't think so," she answered, thoughtfully. "He's just like a dog, sniffing around for the scent after it's gone cold."

"Maybe we should tell him –"

"Leave it to me," she snapped suddenly, looking Pete squarely in the eyes.

The Inspector entered the room. Two policemen now stood just inside the door.

"Good morning, *Señhor. Señhora,*" he inclined his head in a bow, which struck Pete as artificial. "I trust I no inconvenience you in the extreme?"

"Not at all," Amelia said, flatly.

To Pete, it all seemed unreal. His wife was acting a part on the stage, reciting her lines. His role was reduced to that of an extra. The detective was farcical, complete with the requisite ornate uniform, beard and moustaches. It could almost *be* a comedy, save for the sinking feeling Pete felt in his stomach.

They all sat down. The Inspector began.

"*Señhora,* I am pleased to see that you enjoy again the good health – so soon."

Was Pete mistaken, or had there been an emphasis on that last phrase – '*so soon*'?

"*Muito obrigado.*" Amelia held his eyes in her stare.

"*Sim*, is much fortunate, since I must need ask you questions and is good you are no longer inconvenienced with – the sickness," he added, delicately.

"I don't see how I can help."

"*Señhora*, I believe it is only you who can be helping me. You alone."

Amelia was silent.

"We found fingerprints of the man we seek. On the window he forced open. The room *you were in*."

"How interesting," she said in a disinterested voice.

"Yes, I find it very interesting. You say you do not see a man. But I know he comes in the window – his fingerprints do not lie. He goes in the room where you are. There is no where for him to hide – so – think carefully, is possible you did see him, yes?"

Pete fidgeted ever so slightly in his chair. The Inspector stole a quick glance his way.

"Is possible I did see him, *no,*" Amelia emphasized the negative, drawing the Inspector's attention back to her.

The Inspector smiled.

"You, *come se dice*, 'poke the fun' at me there, at my speaking."

Then, on a seemingly different note,

"You think us a very backward people, *não es verdadeiro*, Señhora?"

"Since you ask me bluntly, then yes, it's the truth – *es verdadeiro*. Your airport, for example, was a shambles. Absolutely no security."

"We are not like your City of the Angels, or your New York."

Amelia stifled a laugh.

"You're not even like Little Rock."

"I do not know this Small Rock you speak of; but is possible, yes, that Fíal is smaller and, to you, less important than her. But," his benevolent manner changed here, as he leaned forward and spoke gravely "I have come to speak to you of other things. I have come to give you – *a warning*."

Amelia's eyebrows rose.

"Yes, I see in your eyes you think I am a fool, very pompous. But you choose to place yourself in great danger, *Señhora*. Have a caution."

"Where, exactly, does this 'great danger' come from?" Her tone held a challenge.

"The man you assisted is not a safe person to have met. No, not safe at all. There are many men, men of the least scruples, shall we say, who are now very much interested to make your acquaintance."

Amelia paused.

"Are you one of them?"

"Is true, I have sought out the acquaintance with you, but for the reasons totally different. I can see you enjoy much this game you play; last night, especially, you enjoy making a fool of the police. Yes, *Señhora,* you fool us and have the fun and are very smart. But you do not yet comprehend the *risks.* I feel the responsibility. You are a woman both beautiful and intelligent. I do not want any evil to come to you here."

"Is that a threat, *Señhor Inspector?*"

Gesticulating with his hand, he cried, "No, you have misinterpreted my meaning entirely!"

"Have I?" she asked coolly.

"Yes, a thousand times, yes. I am asking if you will permit me to *protect* you. You are in, as they say, 'pretty deep.' *Por favor*, think before you answer."

Pete had been closely following the conversation; mesmerized, as if by a dramatic performance. Now that there was a momentary pause, he roused himself and turned towards Amelia. He was about to speak, when her answer came in clear, decisive tones.

"I apologize if I have wasted your time, *Señhor.* But you confuse me for someone who can assist you."

De Sousa smiled sadly, and spoke, as if to himself. "So, it is like that, yes? I am sorry".

Then, speaking quickly and assuming a business-like manner, "If you will not give me your trust, *Señhora,* I must give you what assistance I can while you are still on my island. You will be approached; when you are alone, if possible. *Señhor*," here he turned a severe face towards Pete,

"You two must be together at all times. *Together*. Do you understand?"

Pete nodded, but he did not understand.

"*Geralmente* – usually - one man will approach you, alone. Others wait nearby. The man will be nice, very nice. Clean, respectable. He will show you the identification perhaps; perhaps not. He will first tell you story, very good story to make you trust. He will seem very good, even kind. Then, he will begin ask you the questions. *Be cautious of this man.*"

Amelia looked at the Inspector, then smiled.

"I will take your advice," she said, decidedly. "And since you have very adequately just described yourself and your friends here," here she nodded at the men by the door, "I must wish you a pleasant good-morning, Inspector."

De Sousa shook his head, smiling. "You use my words against me a second time, *Señhora*. I pray that the Virgin protect you."

They all rose, de Sousa again bowing stiffly.

"*Returno al estacão*," he barked in a loud voice to his two underlings, who turned and walked out the front door.

"If you are going out, may we offer you a lift into town?" the Inspector inquired, politely.

"Thank you, no," Pete said, as if finally remembering his lines, "We have a rental car."

"Of, course. *Señhora*, if you would be so kind as to permit me the use of your telephone? I have been longer here than I plan, although," here he looked dejectedly at Amelia, "With less success than I hope."

"Right in here."

Amelia showed the Inspector into the back hallway, which housed the sole telephone on the premises.

"Goodbye," Pete said, shaking hands with the policeman.

"Goodbye; the maid can show you out when you're finished," added Amelia.

"*Señhor, Señhora, adeus.*" Again, the stiff little bow, "Remember, in our country that means, 'Go with God.'"

"Uh, thank you," Pete replied, at a loss.

"I'll just get my bag in here, Pete."

Pete walked past de Sousa and out the back door, crossing the courtyard towards the garage. He had flung its doors open, and was fumbling about in his pocket for keys when a sudden, sickly feeling overcame him.

Amelia had not followed him out the back door.

The stretch of courtyard separating house and garage was empty. High above now, the sun burned down relentlessly. Everything was deathly quiet, except for the sound of a far-off cowbell.

The cold certainty that he had left Amelia alone in the house with a strange man, after having just being warned against it, smashed into his consciousness with the force of a freight train. He saw small, black dots floating in front of him; his chest constricted; and, for a moment, he stood rooted in place.

The next second, he was running for the house.

When he was halfway there, Amelia opened the door and stepped out, heading for the garage. She walked without looking up, struggling with her purse zipper. Apparently getting the better of it in the end, she got into the passenger seat and closed the car door behind her. It was a few seconds before she noticed her husband hadn't moved in all that time. She looked up and saw what can only be described as his crazed expression.

Puzzled, she asked, "What happened to you?"

"Nothing," Pete whispered woozily, the blood slowly returning to his head.

CHAPTER FIVE

The next few days seemed strangely anti-climactic. The Franklins circumnavigated the small island several times in their rental car, snapping photos of panoramic vistas from various lookout points. They patronized their favorite restaurants, and discovered some new culinary gems. They even took a day trip to the neighboring island of Píco, named for the mountainous pinnacle that dominated that island's landscape.

But nothing happened.

That is to say, nothing *unusual* happened. And both Pete and Amelia secretly kept thinking it would. The serene weather, the distant church bells, even the friendly denizens of the island themselves all seemed out of place after what they had just experienced. If they had been held up by bandits on one of the tiny back roads, or received a coded message in their breakfast cereal, they would have felt, in some way, *relieved*.

Because it was the *waiting* that was unbearable. Both of them knew, in their heart of hearts, that their part in this story was not yet over.

"We might as well look up Fr. McGinley," Pete suggested one afternoon.

"Your old pastor, from when you were a kid?"

"Yes. Imagine him being stationed out here, in the middle of nowhere. Mom gave me his address; we might as well look him up. Unless," he added, hopefully, "There's something else you'd rather do?"

The five remaining days until they took the small *TAP* (Trans Atlantic Portugal) airliner back to Lisbon now seemed, for some reason, interminable.

"No, that's fine. We've got nothing else to do."

"Okay," Pete sighed, getting out his keys.

To himself, he thought, "Things have definitely changed."

And they had.

For the second honeymoon, despite the date printed on their return tickets, was definitely over. After the night of O Birraca, things had become rather strained. They had not argued again, but somehow, for all Pete's trying, neither had they 'made up'. The very fact that two mature adults, alone on a romantic island and unfettered by the constraints of childcare or career, could find nothing better to do than look up an old parish priest was testimony enough of this fact.

In due course they arrived at the cathedral of São Fortunato.

It was an ancient, towering cathedral with rows upon rows of purple flowers growing in the square out front, running up almost to its very doors. From the heady sunlight, they entered into the perpetual near-darkness of all European churches. They walked towards the front.

Under the main altar, ensconced in an ornate glass coffin gilded with gold, lay what remained of Saint Fortunato's body.

"Oh, let the poor man rest!" was all Amelia could whisper.

Although the Catholic Church boasts many incorruptibles, men and women whose bodies (for unexplained reasons) have escaped the ravages of time and decomposition, Saint Fortunato (unfortunately) was not one of them.

The man had most likely been a kind man; a man so revered, his countrymen had erected this stately memorial around him; a man who had gained renown for remaining unmarred (for a time) after his death. But once the natural processes had begun on his corporeal remains, the townspeople had been loath to part with their local celebrity; or even, it appeared, to give him a Christian burial.

"Oh, it's disturbing! It's not even right," Amelia continued, her hand at her throat.

"It's not *that* bad," Pete ventured, ever the optimist.

"Oh, let's go to a side altar."

They passed up a side altar displaying a mannequin - an actual mannequin, exactly like a department store's - portraying St. Rocco, surrounded by statues of dogs licking his bloody wounds.

"Not much better," said Amelia.

Finally, they came upon a recessed, Rococo-styled alcove, with golden angels hurling themselves in a perpetual orbit around a placid Virgin.

"That's more like it," sighed Amelia, kneeling down on the hard, wooden kneeler.

Both Catholics from their youth, the Franklins now found themselves oddly at ease in this unusual place of worship.

"Why don't you go see if McGinley's in one of those confessionals over there."

She motioned towards the far wall with her head, her hands already joined in front of her on the cold metal railing.

"The sign in the back said - in Portuguese, of course - that confessions were being heard in English from three to four."

Pete glanced at his watch. "It's quarter to four now."

He started to go then stopped, looking unsure.

"Do you think – I mean, do you mind - being left alone?"

She looked all around her at the massive, deserted building. There wasn't a sound.

"I think I'll be alright," she said, smiling. "'Sanctuary,' and all that."

"Well, okay then."

Pete walked off.

Amelia closed her eyes and wearily massaged her forehead with her hand, as she dutifully recited her prayers. She remembered her children; her family; and all those who had died (including the unfortunate inmate of the glass coffin).

But her prayer had quickly become a distracted and a hurried one. Her feeling of security had suddenly worn off, and she now had a strange, sixth sense that something was about to happen. She crossed herself, and sat back onto the creaking pew.

She gasped. Sitting next to her, and looking straight ahead, was the stranger from the other night.

Still not looking at Amelia, he spoke in a pleasant voice.

"They say there are no unanswered prayers," he paused before continuing. "Just prayers we call 'unanswered' because we can't accept the fact that the answer has been 'no.'"

Amelia was still staring at the man. Finally, he turned towards her, placing his arm on top of the pew behind her.

"I thought things were so hopeless the other night, I didn't even bother to pray. But you answered my unspoken prayer anyway. I wanted to thank you for that."

Amelia looked deeply into his chestnut eyes.

"What do I call you?"

He chuckled, "I notice you don't ask what my name is. Very

considerate; you've been well brought-up. I'd be happy if you'd call me Nick. Nick – Adams. That's a good name, don't you think?"

"Fine. And I assume somehow you already know mine?"

"Yes, Amelia." Something in the way he said her name made chills go up her spine.

"Well, it's a little easier in my case, since I only have the one name," she said, lightly.

Nick smiled broadly. He looked like smiling (and laughing for that matter) came easily for him, as if life were good and all trouble inconsequential. Then his face sobered a little.

"I'm sorry if bumping into me the other night has but a damper on your vacation. I noticed the locals have been out to pay you a visit."

"The locals? Oh, yes, de Sousa." Then adding, "They found your fingerprints. Did you know?"

"No. So that's it. I couldn't see how they got on to you. Your performance," here he grinned again, mischievously, "Was impeccable. Are you an actress?"

"Hardly. An adjunct professor. No, that sounds so stuffy. I guess I'm a mom, really."

"I envy you." He looked darkly at the polished marble floor, as if seeing in it some reflection he did not like. "And I'll tell you who I really envy;" he inclined his head meaningfully towards the row of confessionals.

"Thank you very much. You've just given me the highest

compliment that's decent to give to a married woman."

He looked at her questioningly. Then he went on.

"Has anyone else bothered you about me?"

"Not yet."

"'Yet?'"

"The police said someone would come up to me, when I was alone preferably, and try to win my confidence. So far, though, no one has."

"How could they with your husband following you around like a –" he checked himself, then went on; "Have you two *always* been that tight?"

Amelia smiled. "No; just since all this happened. We're actually starting to get on each other's nerves a little. De Sousa impressed upon him the importance of not letting me out of his sight, and Pete's taken it pretty seriously."

"Have you?"

"What? Taken it seriously? Well, I did at first. I kept imagining I was in terrible danger; that my food would be poisoned, or the car blow up or something like that. But things have been fine, a little boring even. To tell you the truth, until I saw you again today, the whole thing was beginning to seem more and more like it never happened."

"Oh, it happened all right."

Why did every casual comment Nick made seem so laden with meaning?

"And I'm afraid that for all your boredom you might still be in danger."

"But why? What do I know?"

"You know me."

"No, I don't; not really. I mean, I know what you look like, and I'd know your voice I again if I heard it and I know one of your aliases. That's it. If I'm to be a marked woman because of some terrible secret you're supposed to have entrusted to me, don't you think, to make it worthwhile, you ought to actually entrust me with one?"

Nick looked bemused. "You have just offered me the single most convincing argument for divulging classified information that I have ever heard. You're amazingly persuasive, you know that? Those eyes, and that delivery! Forget teaching, sister, you should join us."

"Who's 'us'?"

"Now, that would be telling. No, I really can't let you in on this one. Scout's honor. But I do see your point. You've gotten messed up with this thing through no fault of your own. You really *don't* know anything, but no one would believe you. They'd all think you were 'in' on it – and I guess you are, in a way. You – you still have it, don't you?"

"Yes, I keep it sewn up in my scrunchie."

Seeing his confused look, she swung her long ponytail over one shoulder, revealing a band of pink silk. Nick nodded, comprehendingly.

He looked around the empty church, before inclining his

head towards hers and beginning in a softer voice,

"Actually, I didn't come here to give you information, or try to get you further messed up in this whole thing. I came to ask you two questions."

"Okay."

Amelia noticed the momentary flash of sunlight, indicating a door had been opened somewhere. He continued now, quickly; repeatedly looking over his shoulder.

"The first one is, if anything happens – to you, I mean – if anyone tries to; oh God, this is hard. Amelia, I don't want to lose you to them." His face looked strange.

"If anything happens, *what*?" Her voice was commanding.

"Can you – just, tell them you know where it is, but have made contingency plans with Saul."

"I know where *what* is?"

"I can't tell you, or I'd be putting you in even greater danger. You must believe me on that. Just remember the name, *Saul*. Say, if he doesn't meet with you in person right away, 'the errors will be deleted.' Can you remember that? Do you understand?"

He was urgent.

"Of course I can remember. But Nick, I don't know what's happening."

"Neither do I, dear. Neither do I."

Amelia thought she heard a faint, rustling noise far behind them.

Nick slid his arm around her waist, drawing her to him. She was certain he was going to kiss her again, as he had on the first night they met. Instead, still holding her close to his side, he stood up and started walking with her towards the confessionals.

"Quickly," he whispered.

Now there was no mistaking the sound of footsteps from the back of church.

They were half-running as they crossed in front of the main altar. Saint Fortunato remained in his uneasy sleep. His arm still around her, Nick was shoving Amelia forward with each stride. Stifled shouts were heard from their pursuers.

They ran.

Amelia asked, in between breaths, "The second thing?"

Nick was looking behind him as he ran, still pushing Amelia in front of him.

"The thing you wanted to ask me?"

They were gaining on the row of small, wooden cubicles; each with a center door for priest, and two curtained recesses on either side for penitents.

They continued to run. Now, they were nearly there.

"Why," Nick panted, "Why do you trust me?"

And with that, he flung Amelia into one of the curtained recesses. She landed, quite painfully, on her husband. Their heads bumped together with the initial contact; and then, as they slumped down onto the confessional floor, their knees and elbows became unpleasantly jammed in one another's rib cages.

The sound of footsteps and shouts passed them by quite close, and then receded, echoing off the high ceiling.

Awkwardly, they tried to extricate themselves from one another. From the small, ironwork grate came an elderly man's troubled voice,

"Are you alright, my son?"

Pete looked at his wife in the fluttering light. The curtain hung crazily from its rod.

"We're fine, Father."

CHAPTER SIX

They rode back to the villa in silence. They exited the car and walked into the hallway. The house was silent.

Where were the kids? Kids were just what they needed right now; that noisy, rambunctious distraction the Franklins had come to rely on when they needed to temporarily escape from one another's company.

If they had been home, Pete would have taken the boys out back to play catch; Amelia would have helped her daughter with her homework or played dolls. All in the name of duty, of course; of 'good parenting.' They would never have admitted it was also their way of putting off the hard decisions; of not asking the difficult questions.

They wandered around the living area restlessly, desperate for distraction. The maids had done a good job, nothing was out of place ('Nothing for me to tidy up,' noted Amelia, vexedly). They sat down at last, on opposite sides of the room ('Not even a television,' Pete grumbled inwardly).

With nowhere else to turn, they turned and faced each other.

"Can we talk about it?" Pete began at last.

"I don't know if I'm ready to talk about it."

"Come on, Amelia. I've been as patient as I can be," then, checking his rising voice, added, "I promise I won't fly off the handle this time. But what happened out there?"

"I saw him."

"'Him'? The man from the other night?"

"Yes."

"What did he say? Did he try to – to hurt you in anyway?" Pete's color was rising.

"Of course not, Pete. I've already told you, I don't think he's dangerous."

"'Woman's intuition' might be good enough for you, but hell! Amelia, I don't like this situation, not at all. And I don't like this man. *He's trouble and you just can't see it.* I don't know what's come over you lately. You're like – like somebody else entirely."

"Like whom?"

"Just not like Amelia. You were always so nice and simple

and —"

"Boring and frumpy and why don't you go on insulting me, while you're at it."

"'Melia, be reasonable. And don't put words in my mouth. I'm not trying to pick a fight. It's just, ever since you met that man – God, can't you see; I'm desperate, here. Have some pity on a guy. I'm not as good at you as expressing myself, never have been. I just want our old life back. I want the old *you* back."

"There's no going back," Amelia said strangely, staring out the window. "Just forward."

"Then, what do we do? You tell me what to do, because I don't know anymore."

"Are we talking about us now, or about that man?"

"Both, it seems! Every time we start talking about him, we end up talking about us."

"And every time we talk about us, we fight."

Amelia was silent for a while, then went on in an odd voice,

"Maybe we should never have come back here. Ten years is a long time. Things happen in all that time; disappointments and – well, other things. We bury stuff deep down inside ourselves, hoping we never see it again because - that would be too awful."

She turned to Pete, as if she had been far away, and only now realized there was someone else in the room.

"You and I seem to have awoken some things that had been

better off left alone."

Pete stared at his wife. His eyes were red and brimming, but he could not cry. He felt too empty inside.

Then, in a desperate attempt at normalcy, he said, gruffly,

"We haven't eaten all day. Let's go out."

"If you want to."

"I want to," Pete barked.

They left the villa.

* * *

When questioned about it later, they could never remember if they had left the door unlocked.

After an uneventful meal, they had turned onto the drive leading to their villa to see lights flashing. Several compact police vans were parked outside, and men in uniform walked around outside, checking windows and looking in outbuildings.

They were brought inside to utter ruin. The painstakingly ordered interior Amelia had only just been criticizing, lay in pieces and fragments all around them. Plates smashed, tables upturned, upholstery slashed.

Eventually, de Sousa came forward. Gone was the kindly, persuasive gentleman of a few days before. Now, he seemed a completely different man; his whole persona had altered. He was animated, agitated.

Upon seeing them, he immediately began scolding Amelia.

"See what come of you foolishness? You foolishness and

you American obstinacy!"

Amelia went to sit down, but there were no chairs left intact. She stood.

"I give her advice, she ignore. I say to her, 'You are in danger;' she wish me good day. I say, 'Let me help you;' she say, go to hell!"

De Sousa had worked himself into a fervor by now, pacing back and forth like an animal. He angrily dismissed the other officers from the room.

"What will the police find? Nothing! Everything destroyed. Either these men find what you were hiding, and is gone now; or they destroy everything in their madness and will strike again. And next time they come *when you are at home.* Think on that!"

"And you!" He turned a furious face at Pete, "What kind of husband do you have in you country? You wife obstruct the justice; she play with the criminal man like he is a toy; you even let her fall in love with him! And what do you do? *Nada.* Nothing. You stay quiet, like a little mouse. I say, there are no men in US! In our country, a real man would –"

Here Pete interrupted.

"Señhor, we have no interest in what the great Portuguese male would have done in my shoes. You can say what you like about me, or my country; but you go too far when you insult my wife with your accusations - accusations that are unfounded. For all we know, some local burglars broke in

tonight. Drunks, or drug-addicts, or whatever else you have over here. Go find your criminals; stop posturing, and yelling at the victims."

"Victim! He call himself a victim!"

"I am; a victim of your inadequate law enforcement, and of your ridiculous speeches. You have insulted my wife. I would order you out of the place; but as we are obviously not staying in this shambles, *we* will leave for the hotel instead." Looking around, he said, contemptuously, "You're welcome to this dump."

Amelia had seemed in a daze ever since she entered the house. Now, she turned and looked at her husband with a new look in her eyes.

"*Señhor*, you and your wife will do well not to leave the island," de Sousa said, menacingly. "In fact, you will do well not to leave your hotel."

Receiving no answer to this, he raged on,

"We watch you two! We watch you two sneaky Americans! You no fool us!"

Gently picking his way over the broken glass, Pete led Amelia to the door. He turned around just long enough to say,

"Go to the devil."

They walked, arm in arm now, back to their car. Amelia leaned heavily on Pete. No one tried to stop them. Pete got into the seat beside her.

"Okay," Amelia said, answering Pete's question from earlier that evening; "I'm ready to talk about it now."

CHAPTER SEVEN

"Well, do any of them make any sense?"

"Not much."

The Franklins sat on the small, concrete porch attached to their hotel room. In front of them, and three stories down, was a dentist's office, a garbage dumpster and several lines of laundry.

But they hardly noticed the disappointing view; they had other things on their minds.

They had not bothered to go to bed after leaving their desecrated villa. Instead, after booking the first available room in the economy *Hotel Gandalfo*, they had put aside their sweeping personal problems to address their more immediate situation. They began forming possible plans of action; but none of them seemed particularly good, especially after a sleepless night. And neither one could find a plan they both agreed upon.

They agreed they were in some kind of danger. They agreed that the local police had turned antagonistic. They agreed they required some kind of outside help. But beyond this consensus, they were at a loss as to what their next step should be.

"We could leave the island," Pete had suggested first.

"But what if de Sousa is watching the ferries? He warned us not to leave, remember."

"I remember, alright. But I don't know what kind of legal grounds he has for that."

"Well, he thinks I'm obstructing justice. Maybe I was before; but that's because I hadn't made up my mind if I could trust him."

"Well, I'm glad you didn't, after all," Pete said, with feeling. "The man's a complete Neanderthal! Where did he get his police training? From some pulp fiction comic book? *'I watch you sneaky Americans!'*" he mimicked. "Worse than that, he's a Neanderthal with dual personalities. He was nuts last night."

"I guess he *thinks* he's just doing his duty," Amelia

considered, "But he was a bit over the top."

"I'll say."

"Well, alright. He might stop us from getting on the ferry. It only runs twice a day; it *would* be pretty easy to spot us. And there's no airport on Fíal. What alternative does that leave us?"

"Well, if we do end up in legal trouble, it would be good to have some kind of representation," said Pete. "Could we get a lawyer over here, do you think?"

"I wouldn't. Not until we're charged with something."

"What do you mean, '*until* we're charged.' Are you that sure it'll come to that?"

"I'm not sure of anything anymore, Pete."

And around and around it had gone like that, with half-baked notions being proposed and rejected; until, half-asleep in their chairs, they had been roused by knocking at their door.

"I'll get it," Pete had said, rising stiffly.

It was the bellhop – all gold braid and red coat, several sizes too large for him - with a letter for them. Pete tipped the boy, and then tore open the heavy parchment envelope, stamped in gold with *United States Embassy.*

The enclosed letter was written on embossed stationary, and Pete read it aloud.

My Dear Mr. and Mrs. Franklin,
I was shocked and appalled to hear of your grave

inconvenience last night. It is a blight upon our islands, and an unspeakable offense against American citizens traveling abroad. The local police inspector has requested I speak to you about a matter of some urgency, with which he is confident you are cognizant. In any case, I would have insisted upon meeting with you in person to extend my sincere apologies for such an insult upon fellow countrymen. I feel, because of my position, deeply responsible for any outrages occurring against Americans while on our islands. If you have been offended during your stay in the Azores (as I am certain you must be, given the severity of the affront) then I truly have failed at my post. Would you do me the honor of meeting this afternoon at two o'clock, at the Café Belem, 28 Rue Mantega? I shall do my utmost to ensure a safe and satisfactory remainder of your stay with us. With deepest respect, I remain
Sincerely Yours,

Matthew Kent
American Consulate
Azores, Portugal

Holding up the letter, Pete looked, bewildered, at his wife. "Now, what the hell is this?"

* * *

The Franklins arrived at the café. At two o' clock, the place was nearly deserted, due to that great national pastime – the *siesta*. The few outside tables were unoccupied. The enormous shade trees outside the café, poking through inadequate openings in the cobblestone, gave the place a look of semi-twilight. The couple stepped tentatively inside the café.

The interior was glossy mahogany, and even darker than they had expected. The ceiling lights were turned on. A few sailors smoked cigars at the bar. The only other occupant sat alone at a corner table, reading a newspaper.

"Mr. Kent?" Pete inquired as they approached the table.

The man folded the paper and smiled pleasantly.

"Hello, you two."

This was a different salutation that they had been expecting, and caught the Franklins off-guard. Given Kent's effusive letter, they had expected a mousy, effeminate diplomat; gushing words of apology and assurance. Instead, this man was in his early forties; robust; with a dark, bristling crew cut, polo top, khaki cargo shorts and flip flops. Without getting up, he pulled two chairs over and said,

"The Yankee's won the pennant in seven, did you hear?"

The Franklins shook their heads and sat down.

Kent glanced fondly at his *Daily News*.

"It takes a while for the paper to get out here – it comes in on the big military aircraft out on Santa Maria – but somehow it's nice knowing your team's doing well, even if the news *is* a little late. Usually, I keep current by the internet; but my secretary forgot to pay the bill, so mine's down right now," he ended, good-humoredly.

The Franklins still stared at the man. Then Pete spoke, puzzled.

"Mr. Kent, -"

"Matt, please."

"Uh, Matt. You *did* write us a letter, didn't you?"

For response, Kent threw back his head and laughed.

"You were expecting some officious son-of-a-bitch after reading that, weren't you?"

"Well, honestly, yes. You don't speak at all like you write."

"*I* didn't write that epistle. It's all Johnson's - my. secretary's - doing."

"Do you dictate it like that?" Amelia asked, addressing the man for the first time.

Kent turned towards her, his eyes twinkling.

"Good Lord, no! I just said, 'get those Franklins on the line and see if they'll come to lunch. De Sousa's spouting fire about something or other again.' I only read the rough draft, though; I never saw what he finally sent you. Was it pretty bad?"

"It would have seemed natural in a Victorian novel," Amelia commented, "But it was a *little* out of place in real life, I thought."

"*'A little!'* You're too kind. That guy is hopeless. He used to write obituaries, I think; or greeting cards; or was a speechwriter or something like that. Now he's working on his life story – at thirty-one. Who will want to read it, I say? 'The partial life story of a guy who sits around in an office all day'. I tell you, he's completely hopeless. He just sits there at his computer, for eight hours a day, typing. And reading me bits of it – that's the worst!"

He continued in a falsetto voice,

"*'My mother comes into my nursery, smelling of lilac water, and weeping. "We've lost your auntie, dear, to the gout. This will be a true blow to you I know, my darling lamb'* – blah, blah, blah! I used to listen, but now I just cover my ears, or leave the office entirely."

The Franklins found themselves chuckling, despite themselves.

"But why don't you fire him if he's so inefficient?"

"Who said he's inefficient? Best secretary I ever had! Just officious, that's all."

"But if he's writing his story all day, when does he ever get his work done?"

The man roared again. "What work? In case you haven't noticed, my dear, this ain't no Paris or Tokyo – this isn't even DeBuque! Nothing ever happens here; nothing much, that is. Not until you two came along."

He winked at them, impertinently

The waiter came up with menus.

"Put those away, my good man," he bellowed. "Bring me my usual." Then, inclining his head confidentially towards the couple, he said in a low voice, "I've trained them to make a pretty decent burger and fries. Want some?"

They nodded.

"*Tres*, my good man. No, make it *cinco*," he nearly yelled, holding up five fingers in front of the waiter's face, "Mr. Franklin and I can polish off more than one each, I bet."

The waiter retreated.

"The bad part is, it takes them forever to make. No McDonald's here, I'm afraid. You would think he was making a seven-layer cake from scratch. The good part is, however, we have time to talk shop; which is something I don't get to do much. Probably not as much fun for you, but, what can you do."

He put both hands on the table and looked at them, expectedly.

"Well," he said when neither Pete nor Amelia had spoken. "Fill me in."

"Fill *you* in? Don't you know all about it?"

"Nothing."

"But you're an ambassador!"

"Sadly, I am not."

Their smiles vanished; the couple shrank back in their chairs, alarm registering on their faces.

"Who are you then?"

The incorrigible man laughed again.

"No, no. No cloak and dagger stuff. I'm not really a criminal mastermind or anything so romantic. I just meant, I'm not an *ambassador* (although that's what mom tells the neighbors); I'm just the Vice Consul of a teeny-weeny consulate, which isn't the same thing at all. I mean, I do have my ambitions. I'd like to work my way up to, say, the main office in Lisbon (they have a real embassy there). And from there to, maybe, Italy or Norway; someplace not *too* big, but still, a big step up from here. Don't get me wrong; the Azores are beautiful - *for visiting*. But not a lot of Americans visit, so my job's pretty slow. I go out fishing most days. Now, I have a buddy out in the Cairo office, who might go out to the Middle East next. No, way. That's a little *too* much action for me, thank you very much."

Amelia said, "But de Sousa must have said something to you."

"Said something? He wouldn't shut up for half an hour, although I couldn't tell you what he was yapping about. All about how you were 'interfering with a criminal man' and 'obstructing the justice.' Was he ever mad!"

Kent was evidently delighted.

He continued, "He said you helped an American get out of a window; seems the guy was in some kind of trouble. I probably would have done the same thing in your shoes. So, I told him, 'What's the big deal?' And that got him ranting and raving for another half-hour. Personally, he has this thing for me. Thinks my consulate's a joke and all that. Anyway, he says you saw the guy again – in a church, I think – but I didn't see the crime in that either. I mean, de Sousa's a nut case," here he looked quickly around the empty restaurant before continuing *sotto voce*; "Unofficially, of course. So you see, for all the noise this guy made, I really don't see what all the fuss is about; I mean other than your rental villa getting trashed, which really *is* too bad. I'm sure the insurance will pay for it, though," he added, as an after-thought.

"Really, Mr. – I mean, Matt," said Pete, "That's pretty much all that happened. I don't know how we can be blamed for it, really. Even if this guy is wanted by the police for something."

"Neither do I. But de Sousa was adamant that you were helping this guy out in some way. Either giving, or receiving information; or even hiding something he gave you two. That's why, he thinks, your place got trashed."

Kent went on, wearily. "I hate to play the big heavy here; and I hate to admit that, maybe, the fruit-cake has a point. But honestly, if somehow, through no fault of your own, you've got mixed up with this fugitive in some way, the best thing to do *is* to let me help you. I've got friends at the Lisbon office; they can help you a lot more than I can. I can put you in touch with them, or you can call them direct. In the mean time, is there anything I can do to help you?"

"De Sousa said we couldn't leave the island. He put us under 'house arrest,' I think it's called; but we ignored that."

"No, that's ridiculous. He has no jurisdiction over that. He can't keep you here against your will if you haven't been charged with anything; he's just grandstanding - again. No, what I meant was, can I help you with this guy? *Are* you involved with him? Hey, come on; it'll go no further than this table."

The Franklins looked at each other, undecided.

"Is he giving you messages; or did he ask you to hold some item for him, maybe just until he could come reclaim it?"

The Franklins looked again at this representative of their country. It was refreshing (especially as the 'old-world charm' of the islands had begun to wear thin) to enjoy his candor, humor and laid-back manner. This man was normalcy (at least *American* normalcy) personified. And what he was suggesting to them – putting themselves in the hands of competent American diplomats – was the perfect solution to their dilemma. Surely he would have ties with the State Department, Amelia thought. Who better than he to get whatever it was she was concealing into the right hands.

Still, for some reason, Amelia held back.

"Really, there's nothing to tell. I *did* run into this man. I helped him out, once, before I knew he was wanted by the police. And he did follow us to that church; but he didn't tell me anything important."

"What did he say, *exactly*. Remember; it might not have seemed important to you, at the time."

"Nothing. I mean, he just talked about prayers, and how he envied me and my life, and stuff like that."

"No message of any kind?"

Why did the almost imperceptible change in Kent's voice make Amelia hesitant?

"No; no message."

Kent sat back in his chair and smiled.

"That was a *pretty* good lie, Mrs. Franklin; but not quite perfect. Okay. I see. 'Charade.'"

"'Charade?'"

"The movie. With Audrey Hepburn. She meets this guy in the CIA who wants her to help him. But they always meet in restaurants or talk over the phone, so she doesn't know he really doesn't have an office at the CIA because *he's the bad guy*. I'm meeting you at the Café Mantega, so maybe I really don't have a dusty little office and a secretary named Johnson; so you're not talking. Fair's fair."

He leaned back in his chair as he saw the waiter coming out of the kitchen.

"My office is on São Miguel, by the way; they don't have a consulate way out here. But I doubt you would have been impressed by it, either way. Okay, I'll give you a number," here he scribbled on the back of one of his cards. "This is the embassy in Lisbon. You can always call them, if you don't trust me yet."

Smiling, he added, "Can't say I didn't try."

Their sandwiches appeared, covered by mounds of french fries. Kent started whacking the uncooperative ketchup bottle with the deftness of his race. Noticing their stares, he looked up, grinning sheepishly.

"I know," he laughed, "I'm almost too American to be real."

CHAPTER EIGHT

"That's the last of it."

Amelia surveyed the luggage she had just finished packing, now piled high on the bed. They had returned to their villa only long enough to collect what belongings had not been destroyed by the vandals. Now, they were back at the hotel.

"Are you sure it'll be okay?"

"You heard what Kent said. The police can't keep us here if we aren't charged with anything. And I, for one, don't intend on waiting around until de Sousa thinks of some trumped up charge to bring against us."

"Alright. Let's go down to the harbor and see if we can buy our tickets for tonight's ferry in advance. And we can see if they'll keep our stuff behind the desk, in case we need to get out of here in a hurry."

"Okay."

After giving the desk clerk their key (as well as a sizable tip), the couple strolled down to the harbor by a circuitous route.

"Do you think we're being followed?" Amelia queried.

"No."

"But de Sousa said –"

"Never mind that guy. You know, I've finally placed him mentally. Fidel Castro."

"Well, maybe the facial hair –"

"*And* the attitude."

From the tiny side street, they could hear the crying of gulls and feel the breeze freshen in their faces as they neared the harbor.

"Amelia."

"Yes?"

"Can I ask you something?"

"What?"

"Are we okay?"

"Not this again. We've already had this discussion, Pete –"

"I know. But I wanted to ask you again, anyway."

Amelia was thoughtfully silent.

"What is it?" Pete asked.

"I was just thinking. We've been through a lot. Not just recently. I mean, ten years together. The kids, the house, work, everything. Everything we hoped for and didn't get; and all the things we didn't dare hope for, but got anyway."

"Like what?"

"Like - happiness."

"Are you happy, Amelia?"

"Now, or before?"

"Oh, I don't know. You pick."

"Before . . . I don't know. I mean, there were, of course, so many happy times. The babies, and birthdays and trips and all the fun stuff. But, was I generally happy most of the time? I don't know. I think maybe not. I think, I was fighting something all the time. Something I didn't want to believe, or accept, *or be* – it's kind of hard to explain."

"No, I think I know what you mean. Life was good, but could have been better. And the 'could have been better' part always eats at you, and keeps you from enjoying the 'good.'"

"Maybe. Yes, maybe it's something like that."

"And, now -?" Pete left the question open-ended.

"Now . . . You know it's funny. We started out this trip like kids, like we were ten years ago. Just crazy in love; physically attracted to one another; a little bit selfish, greedy even. Greedy for everything. For food, and fun, and excitement – just greedy for *life*."

Amelia laughed.

"Remember, back then, how sensitive we were to everything. How – volatile life was; how volatile *we* were. I mean, if we argued about anything, it would put us back for days, absolute *days*. The fighting, the pouting, the making up – how exhausting it all seems now, in retrospect! People are always trying to 'recapture their youth;' but do they really remember what it was like? The insecurity, the pain, the agony – over *what?* No, you couldn't pay me to go back. For all the arguing we've done on the second half of this trip – the 'grown-up' half, if you will – I'd take that any day."

Pete was curious.

"But why?" he asked, bewildered. "I mean, I loved our honeymoon, and I loved our time before the kids came, and before 'middle age' loomed up ahead of me larger than life."

"I loved those times, too. Don't get me wrong. It's just that, for all their excitement and allure, they also had an undercurrent of – *fear.* Fear that it all might not last. No, it was more than that. I can only describe it as a kind of terror that *we,* as a unit, might not last."

Pete was silent for a moment. They had come out of the dim alleyway into the orange glow of the late afternoon sun, and the bracing wind of the open harbor. They approached the lone ticket booth. There was no ferry at the dock.

"And now," Pete began, hesitantly. "And now you don't feel that? Now you're happy?" He added, almost afraid to ask, but needing to anyway; "*Happier than before?*"

There was no one in line for tickets.

"Yes," Amelia said the world slowly, smiling in disbelief.

"It's crazy, I know, but there it is. I feel we've 'made it,' somehow. Through good times and bad; for richer or poorer; all the things we vowed at our wedding. I guess I was afraid we'd lose our love. But we didn't *lose it* – it just *tempered*. That's the word I'm looking for, I think. It isn't less – it's just changed. It's different, and at the same time, somehow, better. I guess I've just found my place *with you* – I'm not still trying to find it, or fighting against it all the time. Now, even if we argue or disagree – I still feel we've made it. We're – we're not going anywhere. Not without each other, that is. I think the key thing is for me, the fear is gone. In its place is – *permanence*."

"And that's enough?"

Amelia didn't answer.

The ticket window was closed. The dock was deserted. A piece of loose-leaf paper was taped to the window, and fluttered wildly in the breeze. Pete smoothed it out and looked at it. Written in three languages – Portuguese, English and French – were the four words:

'Ferry closed. National Strike.'

"Oh, these socialist countries!" Amelia cried, stamping her foot; the capitalist disgust sounding in her voice.

"You were right, dear. 'We're *not* going anywhere,'" Pete narrowed his eyes, "Not by ferry, anyway."

"What are we going to do now?"

"Don't worry," Pete said, determinedly. "We'll get *somebody* to take us in their boat. Money talks. And, with money, there's no language barrier."

They turned and walked back down the long pier together.

* * *

They stopped at a small, dockside café for a quick meal, and to reformulate their plans. There were no other tourists here, and no amenities; unless you counted the fact that, for an additional fee, they would do your wash while you waited. A few sailors hung about the place; smoking, laughing, horse playing and hauling enormous duffle bags of laundry off their tiny fishing vessels.

"How long do your strikes usually last?" they inquired from the waiter.

The young man hastily wiped down their table with a greasy rag. He had untidy black hair and darting eyes. He wore a dingy white dress shirt (untucked); and a black bowtie which tried, unsuccessfully, to restrain the scrawny man's bobbing Adam's apple.

"Mister, it take one day, two – maybe week. Is no can tell. No bus go, no ferry. Tourist get much anger. We who live here – does no much matter. Where we need go? Is no hurry."

"Uh, yes. But do you think, if I *were* in a hurry, somebody would take me in their boat?"

"Where to?"

"São Miguel; to the airport. I need to get back to Lisbon."

"São Miguel long way, long way in little fishing boat."

"Yes, I know. But *are* there any larger boats available?"

"No, just fishing boats. The big ferry no run now."

"Yes, I know that," said Pete, trying not to sound as frustrated as he was becoming. He spoke very slowly and distinctly.

"So, do you think someone would take me all that way, to São Miguel, in a fishing boat?"

"For money?"

"Of course, for money."

"Then, no problem."

The waiter turned around and started yelling rapidly at the group of sailors. There was a great deal of shouting and cheering going on. One sailor had another one in a neck lock, and from the cash fluttering to the ground, it was apparent that wagering was yet another unadvertised amenity of the establishment. The waiter, although a puny man, nonetheless pushed himself into the fray; still yelling and pointing to the American couple. The man in the neck lock was released with a thud. A great deal of discussion ensured, in several languages; with ample pointing – first from the Americans, to the boats, and then back again. Finally, their waiter returned.

"No problem. He take you."

"Who?"

"Ándre. Is my cousin. Have fast boat, very fast. Best on island."

The Franklins were skeptical of this, but went on.

"What time?"

"Okay, seven. Eight. Does no matter."

"Yes, it *does* matter, to us. We'll be here at eight."

"Okay," he repeated, shrugging as he turned back towards the kitchen to get their order; "Does no matter."

Amelia looked at Pete. "He seemed a little vague."

"They're all vague. Living on an island, they lose all sense of time - or urgency."

"What do you think the boat's like?"

"We'll ask to see it first."

But they were unable to inspect the craft. Seemingly, it was in a dock somewhere, having its oil changed, or maybe its sparkplugs. The waiter had been somewhat hazy on this last point. They also could not interview Ándre, as they would have liked.

"Is no here now. Come back tonight. Is fishing."

"In his boat? I thought his boat was being worked on," and then, "And how do you know he will take us if he isn't even here?"

"Is in different boat now," the waiter offered as explanation to Pete's first question. Then, drawing himself up to his full height of 5"2, he said with dignity;

"I know my cousin take you because *I know*."

With that, he left the check and walked away.

"I wish things were a little more - *normal,*" Amelia began, as they rose from their table.

"I know. The whole arrangement's screwy. But we're not in a normal situation. Who knows how long this strike will last. It could last a week, and if it does, we'll miss our connecting flight home - we're supposed to leave in four days, remember. After a couple of days, it might get really hard to hire any boat. Doing this now really *is* our best bet," Pete finished lamely, but he himself sounded unconvinced.

"Maybe, but I still don't feel right about it."

"Well, we'll meet this Ándre tonight, and take it from there."

* * *

A few hours later, the Franklins were just checking out of the *Hotel Gandolfo* when Inspector de Sousa walked into the lobby.

"*Señhor, Señhora,*" he said quietly as he approached. His whole manner seemed subdued, deflated, less flamboyant than on the previous evening; as if, for some reason, his vitality had been sapped from him.

The couple stared at him but made no response.

"I was informed you are leaving us," he continued, in the same, even tones. "You go, even after I warn you not to."

His voice, despite the words, was not menacing as on the other night; if Amelia had had to place it, she would have said they sounded, somehow, *sad.*

Pete was now quick to respond.

"You cannot stop us, de Sousa. We've been in contact with the American consulate –"

"You have?" the Inspector's voice was incredulous.

"Yes, and you can't hold us if we're not charged with anything; and we're not, so we're leaving."

"The consulate told you that himself, did he?" De Sousa seemed taken aback.

"Yes," Pete gloated, happy he had scored a point against the self-assured inspector; "We're not as stupid as you thought."

The inspector rubbed his beard thoughtfully.

"How do you leave, with no ferry?"

"That's our business," Pete answered, hurriedly.

De Sousa turned to the manager behind the desk, and quickly asked him a question in their native tongue. Before Pete could protest, the man obligingly answered, "Ándre."

The Franklins now remembered (and regretted) having asked the manager if he had known a certain Ándre, a fisherman they had hired to take them off the island in his boat.

Pete now glared furiously at the oblivious innkeeper, who had returned to his papers.

"Ándre?" the inspector half-yelled, half-laughed. "Ándre? The man is a drunk! Always I find him in my station, in trouble. He get drunk and his boat, it hit one of the fancy yachts. Much trouble. He lazy man, no good, no reliable."

"Inspector," began Pete, indignantly, "I am sure, at this point, that you would say anything about anyone to persuade us not to leave. Now, that we know you have no *legal* grounds to do so."

"I am tempted to arrest you, if only to keep you from killing yourself on the rocks with this *trafulha!*" the inspector said, exasperated. "To cross to São Miguel is no easy thing in a good boat with a good captain. With Ándre, you will have neither."

"Our minds are made up. We are leaving tonight."

"*Tonight?* In the dark? In that *barco quebrado*? Tcht!" he made a disgusted noise in his throat.

The inspector was silent for a moment. Then he turned to Amelia. His manner was once again ingratiating, his voice persuasive once more.

"*Señhora*, you and I, we have, *come se dice*, hit it off on the wrong feet, have we not? But now, things are serious. *Very serious*," he emphasized, looking intently at Amelia. "If what you husband tell me is true, you are in more danger now than before. You and I, we must put aside our arguing, yes?"

He went on, earnestly.

"I will tell you. There are men here that my police have spotted; men I do not like to see on my island. They escape us at every turn. These are bad men – I do not know who pays them - but they have only one purpose when they appear. They are the killers *professionál*. Many countries wish arrest them. But they are too tricky to get caught."

He learned even closer to her face, as if trying to sway her by the sheer force of his personality.

"You have had much displeasure that my men follow you, I know. They tell me what you do and where you go – that you try to leave island, that you maybe try go by boat. But one reason the police follow you is also to protect you, in case these bad men have come here *because of you*."

Pete scoffed.

"Good try, de Sousa. But it won't work. You really are a first class manipulator. First you tried smooth-talking us, that first day we met you. Classic. Then, since that didn't work out for you, you switched your tactic to bullying us, on the night of the break-in. Now, you're suddenly our friend and ally, our only defense against an imaginary enemy. *'Oh, stick close by me, it's your only hope!'*" he mocked. "That would make trailing us much easier, wouldn't it?"

The Inspector looked defeated. He sighed wearily. Looking directly at Amelia, he said,

"If you go tonight, my men cannot watch you any longer, *Señhora*."

"Thank goodness for that!" Pete piped up.

"If you think I am a sham, I cannot help that, *Señhor*," he said sternly to Pete. "But, *Señhora*, I have given you the warning. I have given you the advice. I have offered you the help. Now is the time you *have* to take it. There will not be a 'later.' You have now to decide if you trust me or not. Do you understand what I say?"

His eyes burned with an inner fire, becoming almost hypnotic in their intensity.

"I understand what you say," Amelia replied, slowly, almost drowsily. Her eyelids drooped slightly, and she turned away from the inspector.

"Well, I don't," Pete said, briskly. "And we'll be leaving now, so we won't have time to figure out your cryptic messages, will we? Boy!" Here he snapped for the bellhop, who started to lug the larger pieces of luggage out to the waiting taxi.

"Goodnight, Inspector," Pete said, trying unsuccessfully to hide the satisfaction in his voice.

"*Boa noite, Señhor.* Safe voyage," de Sousa replied, formally.

Amelia roused herself.

"Goodnight, Inspector," she said with decision, holding her head up high.

"*Boa noite, Señhora.*"

Amelia took one step down the carpeted flight of stairs in front of her, but her heel caught on the luggage strap of one of the carry-on pieces the bellhop had left on the landing. She stumbled, regaining her footing by the third step, but not before crying out in pain.

"My ankle!" she moaned, reaching for her foot.

"Not your *ankle!*"

As the husband of an avid runner, Pete knew all too well that Amelia's body was steel from her head to her knees, and glass from there on down. She had been warned by her doctor to stop running the 5K if she wanted to avoid surgery by 35; the month he told her that, she had competed in the 15K for the first time. Now, as he bent down to support his wife, her face writhed in agony, Pete wondered how many similar injuries lay ahead of them both.

"*Señhora*, is it the foot? Can I be of assistance in the least?"

"No, I'm handling this, Inspector. You've done enough damage," Pete said, roughly pushing past him as he carried his wife to a nearby chaise. "I think I've already said '*goodbye*' to you," he ended, meaningfully.

"It is goodbye, then," de Sousa replied meekly, looking over his shoulder as he left the building.

The fish shop next door provided the necessary ice, and the hotel's first aid kit (when finally located) actually contained adequate bandaging. In fact, there were so many interested bystanders - the manager, his wife, their three kids, the apologetic bellhop, even the fishmonger – all eager to point, prod, give direction and generally enjoy the excitement, that Amelia had to sit a little distance apart from them, at one of the room's old-fashioned writing desks, and have Pete keep the well-intentioned crowd at bay.

While Amelia painstakingly wrapped and rewrapped her

ankle, the onlookers contented themselves with making predictions – perhaps a double fracture? Or even the delightful prospect of a lengthy and expensive hospital stay?

Amelia called out to Pete, who helped her get (gingerly) to her feet, much to the disappointment of the crowd.

"*Señhora*, may we call the ambulance?"

"No, thank you," Amelia replied, wincing. "It's just a sprain."

"But, *Señhora* –"

"I'll be fine. I've just taken some ibuprofen." Then, seeing the last word had not made it through translation, she pulled out the small bottle she had just replaced in her handbag, and shook it for effect, "*Medicina*. So I'll be okay in a couple of minutes."

"Are you sure, 'Melia?" Pete now asked, concerned.

"Positive. I'm actually feeling a *little* better already."

"Do you need the doctor, at least?" the manager inquired, hopefully.

"No. If there's one thing I have a lot of experience at," here she smiled wryly, "It's wrapping my own ankles. Pete, let's go," she said, turning to her husband. "It's almost eight."

"You sure?" Pete asked again, solicitously.

"Be serious," she laughed. "Depending on who you talk to, I'm either in cahoots with a murderer; being pursued by assassins; wanted by the police for questioning, or all of the above. A sprained ankle is the least of our worries at this point."

"Still – " he began.

"I know. It's adding injury to insult. What else is new?"

And with that, she wobbled out to the taxi on Pete's arm.

* * *

After their own misgivings, misfortunes, and de Sousa's dire predictions, they had half expected the dock to be empty at the appointed time.

But as the taxi dropped them off at five minutes after eight, a lone fishing boat – slightly battered, but apparently seaworthy, bobbed complacently on its rope tether at the end of the long pier. They paid the driver (who had already taken out their luggage) and got out.

As they approached the boat (Amelia hobbling slightly less as the pain-killer began to kick in), they were hailed by the waiter of earlier that evening. He was now stripped down to a cut-off tee shirt, boxer shorts and a pair of flip-flops. He had been busy scurrying around the deck, tightening ropes and adjusting valves.

"Hello, Mister. I get you luggage."

"That's alright. Is Ándre here?"

"Yes, below. Adjusting."

"'Adjusting' what?"

"Just getting ready to go. I get you luggage." And with that he was off.

There had still been no sign of his cousin by the time the

waiter returned with his heavy burden. He had decided to carry all six pieces of luggage at the same time, and resembled a pack mule, sweating and straining under the sheer weight of it. Half stumbling, he disappeared below deck with their bags.

"Is everything okay?" Pete inquired, when he finally reappeared, rubbing his dirty hands together.

"Is fine. We go soon."

"When?"

In response, the waiter turned and yelled down the short flight of steps.

Ándre appeared slowly, rising almost majestically out of the dark; he momentarily regarded the Franklins, without apparent interest.

"*Boa noite*," he mumbled indistinctly, rubbing his hands – black with oil and grease – on his already stained undershirt. He was fiftyish and stocky, with an enormous barrel for a stomach. He had deep set, tiny black eyes and a massive jaw. He was dressed identically to his cousin, minus the flip-flops. With a surprising agility, he jumped to the dock and squatted over a dirty sheet, which was littered with innumerable parts and tools arranged in some indecipherable order. Muttering to himself, he took two small pieces, brushed past the Franklins, re-entered the boat and disappeared below deck.

"What is he doing?" Amelia asked, hopping awkwardly to readjust her weight.

"Just touch up - tune out - no, no *'tune-up,'* I think is the word. Make boat *fast!*" he added with a flourish of his hands, the excitement sounding in his voice.

"I thought it was already fast. And anyway, this isn't a race. I just want to get to São Miguel in one piece."

"Is fine. Is best. Okay. No worry."

And after giving this last admonition, the waiter went below to assist his brethren.

Pete helped Amelia sit down on a sawhorse bench someone had left on the dock, and then joined her.

They waited.

They had been talking so much during the past few days – making and reformulating plans, deciding what their best course of action should be – that they now found themselves sitting side by side in silence. Every now and then, they would break that silence by assuring each other that, "We made the right choice," or "This plan we're following really *is* the best;" or Pete would inquire after her ankle; but that was all.

Time passed.

Every once and a while, Ándre or his cousin would come up to rearrange their trinkets on the sheet, or actually take one with them when they returned below. Ándre spoke no English, and his Portuguese was of a variety not found on Berlitz tapes. So all the Franklin's inquiries were directed at the waiter/make-shift first mate, who continually assured them they would be 'departing momentarily,' an English phrase of which he seemed inordinately proud to be able to pronounce.

The incessant lapping of the water against the concrete pier was mesmerizing. Amelia yawned heavily, as a nearby church chimed ten times. Pete checked his own wristwatch for confirmation.

As he stared dreamily in front of him, his gaze fell, for the hundredth time, on the grimy sheet.

He started.

"My God, Amelia. *That's* the engine!"

It was only too true. In his zeal for a better and a faster boat (and influenced by who knows what else), Ándre had chosen this particular evening to disassemble the entire engine, and was now painstakingly reconstructing it, piece by piece. The fact that two Americans had hired him to take them out in his boat on the same night did not seem to worry – or even concern him - in the slightest.

After withstanding the initial onslaught of Pete's invectives, the waiter was apologetic, but as reassuring as ever.

"Is no worry. Ándre fix boat. He remember where every piece go. Is no problem."

"It's a damn problem! I hire him to take me out in his boat; not for him to take his boat apart! This is ridiculous. Get my luggage out of there. The deal is off."

"*Não, não, Señhor*," he whined, rubbing his palms together feverishly. He appealed to his cousin for help, a flood of Portuguese dialect filling the air.

Pete was opening his mouth to begin again, when Ándre raised his hand, commanding silence. His cousin translated the deep, guttural words.

"Ándre wants to know, when you plane leave Lisbon."

"What the hell! What is he talking about? I wanted to leave here *tonight*. You two are -"

"Please, *Señhor*. He is asking me."

"This is insane. I can't believe this is happening," Pete laughed, crazily. Then, too exasperated to say anything else, he turned and shouted directly at Andre, holding up four fingers, "Four days - *quatro dias.*"

Again, Ándre spoke in calm, unemotional tones. His cousin translated.

"Then, *Señho*r, Ándre gives you his word he will get you there in time."

And then, with all the indifference of a king returning to matters of state, Ándre turned around and went back to his work.

The Franklins had been dismissed.

"This is unbelievable. Amelia, we're not waiting here any longer."

"Our luggage?"

"Oh, what the hell. Leave it for tonight. I have to help you; and anyway, I don't feel like lugging it all back." Looking scornfully at the two men, he added, "It's obviously not going anywhere."

"*Não, Señhor*. We watch the bags. They no go anywhere. We fix boat. No problem. Leave tomorrow, day after at latest. We come get you at hotel. No matter. No worry."

And with his high-pitched voice still following them down the pier, for the second time that day the Franklins walked away (albeit this time somewhat more unsteadily), together.

CHAPTER TEN

The Franklins were given their old room. Pete put the small toiletry bag (which he had run back down the pier to dig out of their luggage) on the bathroom counter, but it was never opened. The couple collapsed on the second-rate bed, not even noticing the feel of the springs poking up through the mattress. Exhausted from their ordeal, they fell asleep almost immediately, their clothes still on. Amelia hadn't even unwrapped her ankle.

When Amelia awoke to the feeling of a meaty hand being clamped down over her mouth, and her arms and legs being pinned, it seemed like a continuation of the disturbing dreams she had been having of late. Although her body mechanically struggled to free itself, her mind was on another plane. She felt detached, and on some level actually *relieved*; as if she had known all along that this moment would come. As she was hauled from her bed, still biting and kicking fiercely, her mind was strangely calm. The burdening anxiety she had been experiencing – about what would happen, and when - was now gone. In its place was mindless action.

Amelia tried every self-defense technique she had learned at school, but to no avail. In her college PE class, she had been matched against other people of her size and skill level. Here, almost at once, she knew the situation was hopeless. Her opponent now was no scrawny freshman, but two burly men, easily 300 pounds apiece; gagging her and tying her hand and foot. When she saw Pete's trussed body fall heavily to the floor, unconscious; and his assailants come over to her side of the bed, she gave up fighting altogether.

In a frighteningly short period of time, the couple had been thrown into a laundry cart, wheeled out of the hotel and whisked into a waiting car; driven down deserted streets; and finally hauled onto a waiting speedboat. Pete's body remained motionless, lying on the thick, wet coils of rope that covered most of the boat's small deck.

But Amelia felt extraordinarily alert.

As the engine roared into life and the small craft jumped out to sea, Amelia's senses thrilled. All the lights in town, which were growing smaller by the minute, seemed to twinkle with an unbearable beauty. The cold wind lashed at her body, making her skin prickle and her nostrils flare; filling her whole being with indescribable energy. She noticed long, silvery flashes rising just above the water's surface; and before she could place them mentally, half a dozen flying fish sailed over the boat's hull, one smacking directly into Amelia's cheek with invigorating wetness. As the dark-clothed, faceless brutes sped her towards certain danger and possible death, Amelia Franklin had never before felt so very much alive.

* * *

Even to someone not intimately familiar with Azorean geography, it was apparent they were making for the island of Pico, the island closest to Fíal; separated from her sister by only a small stretch of ocean. As they pulled closer to the harbor, Amelia could just make out the high, twin steeples of the main church; which, during the day, drew one's eye up towards the towering peak which dominated the whole island. Amelia remembered again the articles she had read back in her college library; articles about how Pico boasted the highest point in all of Portugal; and about how an airplane, disoriented by the mist, had once careened into that same island's unforgiving summit.

They passed by the last of the harbor lights, and the engine slowed abruptly as they pulled to the right side of the island.

In pitch-blackness now, the boat nudged slowly forward, looking for some hidden cove or inlet. At last, there were voices from shore, and a dim lantern was visible, swaying back and forth in signal. She heard, rather than saw Pete's body as it was shoved aside, as ropes were cast out to unseen hands. The boat hit something with a shock. Amelia was lifted up effortlessly by the grunt men, who jumped to shore and started on a long, up-hill path. The night was overcast. All she could make out were the dark masses of the men immediately around her; and, far away, tiny boat lights shining out at sea. She heard the wind whistle through tall, dry grass; and the rustling sound of some small night animal. None of the men spoke.

Finally, a small, hard, bright light shone high above them on the path, and the men trotted tirelessly towards it. As they drew nearer, Amelia could see the light came from a white shack on some kind of platform; to Amelia, it looked like the tiny building was on stilts. Intermittently, a painful, groaning noise filled the air. They were almost at the metal ladder leading up to its trap door before Amelia knew what it was. They were going into a windmill.

Once inside, the Americans were thrown to the floor, unceremoniously. The room was larger than Amelia had estimated from outside. It was round, with wooden stairs leading to an upper level. There were a few discarded burlap sacks in a corner, and an old, brown glass bottle. Everything was dusty, and smelled vaguely of grain. Every few seconds, Amelia would feel the room shudder, and hear the moan of mechanisms turning despondently beneath her. The room was illuminated by the powerful halogen lamp she had seen through the tiny, unglazed window high above her. The air was filled with hundreds of moths and other night insects, all pouring through the opening and madly hurling themselves at the lantern in an insane orgy of delight.

Their abductors had deposited the Franklins on the floor and immediately left by the same trap door through they had come. For all her heightened awareness, she doubted if she could now give an accurate description of them. She had only seen their faces for a few seconds, when the trap door had been flung open, and while her eyes had still been readjusting to the light. The men had seemed specifically handpicked for their non-distinctiveness – all seemed to have large, blunt features; small, beady eyes; a stocky, heavy-build and short cropped, brown hair.

Now the Franklins were alone.

Amelia crawled to Pete on her elbows, the gag cutting uncomfortably into her mouth. She nudged him repeatedly, but he didn't move. The only sign of life was the shallow rise and fall of his striped shirt. Amelia managed to sit up, but was bound too tight to stand. She listened intently but heard nothing.

Time passed.

Pete added an occasional moan to that of the windmill as he slowly and painfully regained consciousness. Intently, Amelia watched his eyes flutter. Finally, they opened; at first uncomprehendingly, and then focusing on her. Neither could speak because of their gags. Pete was still too shaken to sit up; so he wriggled as close as he could get to his wife and lay on his back on the hard boards, staring up at the glaring light and watching the dizzying flight path of the insects.

As the two captives sat bound and gagged in the deserted windmill on that tiny island, a sudden thought came to Amelia.

It was after midnight; so that made *today* their anniversary.

* * *

Slowly, the halogen lamp appeared to grow dimmer as the square of sky Amelia could see first turned a pale, and then a vivid, cerulean blue. Day had come.

Amelia looked down at Pete. He had fallen into a fitful sleep, his head now on her lap. His face was patched with bruises from last night's struggle; his left eye was swollen shut.

Suddenly, the trap door was swung open and the morning sun (newly risen over the Atlantic) flooded the tiny room, blinding Amelia for a moment. With the noise, Pete jerked awake and struggled unsteadily to a sitting position. Two strangers, young men shabbily dressed in the local fashion, entered the room and hurriedly cut the Franklin's bonds and removed their gags. As soon as the youths were done their work, they turned and disappeared out the door, after first motioning for the couple to follow.

Amelia worked and reworked her mouth muscles, trying to regain sensation. Pete painfully rubbed his wrists and his ankles; then, his fingers gingerly explored the new, bumpy terrain of his face. When Amelia spoke, her voice sounded strange and her tongue felt too big for her mouth.

"Are you okay, Pete?"

"Just 'okay.' You?"

"I'm not hurt. Just sore from the rope and gag."

They laboriously got to their feet.

"You ready?" Amelia asked, pausing in front of the open door.

"Ready as I'll ever be."

"Pete," Amelia started, looking intently at her husband's face. She seemed about to say something more; then, apparently changing her mind, simply said, "You look awful."

Pete began to smile wryly, then winced in pain.

"Let's go."

Amelia descended the short ladder and found herself in a high, open space overlooking the sea. Her eyes squinted from the sun, and from its dazzling reflection on the water. There was a strong wind coming up from the ocean; she could just hear the booming of the waves crashing far below her, out of sight. She was on a dirt path, which snaked though the scruffy grass; coming up from somewhere below, passing the old windmill and leading uphill to several dilapidated farm buildings. The path Amelia was on was cracked and dry, packed hard beneath her bare feet. Crumbling fencing lay in a shambles all about her. Several scrawny chickens scratched busily nearby.

As Pete descended the ladder, the two youths emerged from one of the outbuildings and came towards them. They now had small caliber rifles slung over their shoulders, the kind used to kill hawks. Seen up close they seemed little more than boys. Whether they could understand the Franklins or not, they made no reply to the couple's demands. They simply escorted them to the nearest farm building, stood outside the door and motioned with their weapons for the couple to enter.

Inside, the Franklins found themselves in an cavernous, abandoned barn. The green, corrugated plastic roof above gave an unhealthy glow to the sheet-metal walls and dark interior. Rows of wooden feeding stanchions and water troughs had long ago been ripped up and removed; only ranks of old water pipes, sticking up eerily from the floor and now leading nowhere, remained of what must have once been a busy (albeit primitive) milking facility.

As their eyes adjusted to the duskiness, they noticed they were not alone. Coming towards them with brisk steps was a man they had never seen before. He was impeccably dressed in suit and tie; his neatness at direct odds with his ramshackle surroundings. As he came nearer, he pulled over two overturned crates and placed them (making certain they were symmetrically spaced) in front of the couple. He snapped, and the two men came in from outside and stood next to him, brandishing their guns. Motioning towards the boxes, he said one word; "Sit."

The Franklins obeyed.

Looking the couple over cursorily, the man began.

"Let's begin, then. I *hope* you are planning on being reasonable." His voice betrayed an English accent, devoid of any emotion. He was bald, of indeterminate age, with a grayish, pocked face.

Neither Pete nor Amelia responded.

"I'll take that as an affirmative, then. Alright. You already know what we want. It's just a question of how unpleasant things have to get before you give it to us. You know you *will* give it to us, in the end."

His calm voice and dispassionate confidence was disconcerting.

"I don't know what you're talking about," Pete began.

"I dare say *you* don't, and I will thank you to stay out of this entirely. I was addressing your wife," was the curt reply.

"'Melia, tell him you don't know what he's talking about, either," Pete implored.

Amelia was silent, staring at the well-dressed man with a shrewd look in her eyes.

"Amelia!" Pete begged, "Be reasonable!"

"Well," asked the stranger, impatiently; ignoring Pete's outburst, "What will it be? I have a plane to catch this afternoon. *Will* you be cooperative?"

Amelia glanced once more at her husband, before replying in a hard, business-like voice Pete had never heard before,

"Of course I'll cooperate. What else can I do? I have to admit, you've got the upper hand here - *momentarily* that is."

"I've no idea what you mean by that last comment, unless it is just more of that wonderful American *bravado* we are constantly subjected to in the cinema. In either case, I'm glad you intend to cooperate; and not just for myself. There are many parties concerned here, as you know; parties who will be eminently pleased to have a satisfactory conclusion to this - messy affair."

"Pete really doesn't know anything about this."

"So I gathered. But it's much the same to me, though. You can't expect me to let him go – not now."

"No, I guess not."

During this entire dialogue, Pete had stared, openmouthed, at his wife. He had gazed dumbfoundedly in front of him, shaking his head in incredulity. But now, his body stiffened. He was no longer the passive victim, doomed to his fate, relegated to the background of this drama. He had just seen something, something that represented a *chance*, albeit a slight one.

Pete Franklin decided to act.

He sprang to his feet, barreling into the slight youth with his middle-aged head. The boy, taken by surprise, sprawled to the ground, trying to curse but finding he had no breath. In another moment, the second boy had jumped on Pete's back, and was yanking his head back painfully when a shot went off. All three wrestling males disengaged and fell apart, panting and staring at the well-dressed man. He now held a pistol in his hand, which he had just fired up into the roof. There was a bright point of light overhead, from where the bullet had penetrated the green canopy; particles of dust and debris, highlighted by the sun, swirled down on the dazed assembly.

"Return to your seat, Mr. Franklin," the stranger said in cool, even tones. "If I had not received instructions to keep you alive - for the time being - that hole would be in your head instead of the roof. However, I sometimes have trouble remembering instructions – temporary memory loss, my doctor calls it. And, if that happens – well, it *would* be too bad for you."

The tackled youth rammed the butt of his rife into Pete's stomach, who cried out and fell at Amelia's feet. The man in charge barked something at him, and the two men drew back.

"I'm going to leave you two for a few minutes. Give you a chance to talk things over. When I come back, I expect you to be ready to give me what I want. Otherwise – well, I think my two friends will be more than happy now to give their full attention to you first, Mr. Franklin; and then to your lovely wife."

He left them. Pete had remained curled up in a ball at Amelia's feet; but as soon as he heard to barn door slam shut, he immediately sat up.

"Amelia! I've got it!" he whispered excitedly.

"Pete, why did you do that? You're crazy. It'll only antagonize them more, and -," she paused, "You've got what?"

"His phone!"

"What? Whose phone?"

"The kid I tackled. It struck me as funny. This kid all got up in peasant clothes, with a cell phone sticking out of his belt. I jumped him just to get it and I did. *I did it,* Amelia."

The pride resounded in his voice. Amelia looked uncertain.

"That was pretty risky, Pete. You could've been shot; you nearly were. But, who do we call? Do you think they have a kind of 911 out here?"

"I've got a better idea." Pete, despite his recent injuries, was smiling assuredly. "Everyone seems to assume I'm some kind of ass or something. But I'm not quite totally daft yet. You remember that card Kent gave us? The one with his cell number?"

"You don't still have that?" Amelia gasped, wide-eyed.

"No. That's back in my wallet in the hotel – unless they stole that, too. No, I anticipated maybe needing it sometime," here he flipped open the phone and started to dial, "So, I *memorized it*."

It was Amelia's turn to stare openmouthed.

Pete paced impatiently back and forth. "It's hard to get a signal up here. No, no wait," here he froze in place, "I've got it."

Amelia glanced nervously at the still closed door. It seemed an eternity before she heard Pete say,

"Hello, Kent? Is that you? This is Pete Franklin."

The silence on her end was unbearable. "I've got to hear. Put it on speaker, Pete. Low."

Pete pressed some more buttons, and the speaker feature engaged, producing a groggy and irate voice on the line.

"What the -, is this your idea of a joke, Tony? Do you know what time I crawled into bed last night – I mean this morning?"

"Mr. Kent, this is Pete Franklin."

"I don't care who the hell it is, I was asleep and – Pete *Franklin*, did you say?"

"Yes."

"Not – no wait. I'm half asleep still. Did you just call me?"

"Yes," Pete said desperately. "Listen. We're in terrible trouble. We need help. We've been kidnapped and we're –"

"– We're on the island of Píco. Up high, someplace. Near a windmill," Amelia finished.

The voice on the other line was a little more alert now.

"*Kidnapped*, did you say? This is incredible. Have you called the police?"

"No, not yet. I don't trust them, anyway," Pete went on. "I memorized your number in case I'd need it; now I guess I'm lucky I did."

"Damned lucky, I'd say. But I think we *should* get the police in on this one; kidnapping is big, and most of our police are trustworthy - really they are. I'll call someone I know in the force, and get the local police on Píco out looking for you, too. Can you be a little more specific about where you are, though?"

"We came by night, and I was knocked out. Amelia?" Pete asked, handing her the phone.

Amelia spoke quickly. "I know we went around the right side of the island, but that's about it. Look for a windmill somewhere on the east, or north-east coast of the island; we're right next to it, locked up in some outbuildings."

Pete grabbed back the phone. "But you have to hurry, Kent. We're running out of time. They're threatening to hurt us both if we don't give them what they want."

The couple heard the barn door open, and could see the dark shape of a man, silhouetted against the bright sunlight, approaching them.

"What do they want?" came Kent's voice on the phone.

"My God; they're coming. Kent, I don't know *what* they want!"

"Ask your wife."

"What'd you say? The reception's bad here."

"I said, *ask your wife*. She knows."

"What do you mean, Kent?"

"Stop calling me Kent."

With an eerie chilliness, the couple realized that the last phrase they had heard came both from the phone in Pete's hands and from the figure now standing in front of them.

Smiling politely, and folding up his phone and replacing it in his vest pocket, was Vice Consul Matthew Kent.

CHAPTER ELEVEN

"You!" Pete gasped.

"Yes, me. You'll forgive me if I had to have my bit of fun with you there. It was too tempting, what with you actually calling me, and all. Bit like a pulp fiction novel, that."

He snatched the cell phone away from Pete.

"Manuel will have to be a bit more careful, what? You might have actually called the police."

"You're English, too," Amelia observed.

"I choose to be English today; yesterday I was an American; tomorrow – who knows? I adopt the persona that best fits my needs; but men like me never really have a nationality. But you know all that already."

"We don't know –" Pete began.

The spurious diplomat held up his hand impatiently.

"Peter, Peter. Please. I've already heard all about your ignorance from Stevenson. He said he very nearly had to shoot you, you were so pig-headed; not a good idea to annoy that man. Personally, I don't know, nor do I particularly care what information your wife may have divulged to you. Your primary value (and, incidentally, the only reason you are still alive) is your usefulness to me as a bargaining chip. Your wife has information we want, and has been terribly reticent about it. Maybe watching her husband's head get bashed in will help loosen her tongue."

The door opened again, and the two youths shambled forward. Their sleeves were rolled up and they were holding nightsticks.

Pete swallowed hard, then got to his feet.

"For the last time, Mrs. Franklin. I am getting tired of waiting."

Amelia was silent. One of the thugs pinned Pete's arms behind him; the other readied his stick.

Pete looked directly at Amelia.

Finally, she spoke.

"Alright. I know where it is. But - I have made contingency plans with Saul. If I don't meet with him right away, in person, *the errors will be deleted."*

"What?" Pete asked in an incredulous whisper.

Kent drew out a handgun and handed it to Manuel, saying nonchalantly, "If he says another word, shoot him."

Then, to Amelia, "That's very interesting what you say there. Very interesting indeed. Why, in fact, this changes everything."

He covered his mouth with his hand, as if momentarily lost in thought. All Amelia could see were his narrowed eyes; she could not read the emotion (if, indeed, there was any) behind them.

Suddenly, his manner was brisk once more.

"You must go. At once. Saul cannot be left waiting."

He helped her to her feet. Amelia looked suspiciously at the man, whose eyes were averted. What was the emotion he was hiding from her? She could feel it emanate from him; his hand was trembling as he held her arm. He seemed as if he were bottled up; ready to explode.

"Pete?" she asked.

"Oh, bring him along, by all means," came the reply.

They were now all hurrying down a passage at the rear of the building, which lead to more abandoned stalls and archaic milking equipment. Kent stopped in front of a wooden door, switched on an overhead bulb and drew back the bolt. He threw the door open with a flourish.

In the dimness beyond, Amelia could just make out old metal

milk canisters lining the walls. Apparently, this had once been a cold storage area of some kind. Now it was covered in dust, and smelled even mustier than the rest of the disused facility. Amelia was about to turn away, when she gasped. A low moan had riveted her attention to a dark figure on the ground. Lying in a heap, and bound with rough cords, was Nick Adams.

"Sorry to disturb you, Saul. But this young woman insists she has an appointment with you."

* * *

"Saul?" Amelia asked in a weak voice.

Her antagonist was laughing heartily. It reminded her of their first meeting at the Café Mantega, when his joviality had seemed so attractive. Now, it repulsed her.

"Good try there, really, Mrs. Franklin" he said, still chuckling. "And if I didn't already have Saul under lock and key, it might very well have worked. I couldn't risk you making any more trouble for us, could I, Saul?" Here he kicked the man on the ground. Another moan ensued.

"Oh, well. I've had a good laugh, though. Now, back to business. Saul was obviously your contact, but now that that's over and done with - "

Amelia interrupted him.

"My *contact?* My God. He was more than that. He was – my lover." And with that, she flung herself down on the floor.

"Have they hurt you? Oh, my love," she was frantically kissing his head, in between sobs; alternately rocking him in

120

her arms and tugging vainly at his bonds.

"Let him go, you beasts!" she hissed, desperately. "You've hurt him. Give him back to me, and you can have whatever you want!"

Saul said in a trembling whisper, "Amelia?"

Then, "What are you saying?"

"I don't care! It's not worth it! Let them have it. We can get away, just the two of us. Nothing else matters, not really."

"But, Pete –"

"Forget all that now. He knows. They all know," she laughed hysterically through her tears. "It's alright, darling. It'll be better now; we won't have to *pretend* any longer."

She was still struggling, unsuccessfully, with his bonds.

The man formerly known as Kent cleared his throat.

"Ahem, madam. It seems I miscalculated when I thought I could use your husband as collateral; it appears you affections lie elsewhere. But, I say, isn't this a bit hard on the chap; I mean, making love to another man right in front of his eyes? It's not the nicest thing to see, right before getting popped off."

"I don't care, do you hear me?" Amelia nearly screamed. "I'm beyond all that; beyond caring." She turned, still kneeling and holding Saul tightly to her breast, and faced the other men. "Do you have any idea, what it's been like? Any idea at all?"

She smiled crazily, stroking Saul's hair tenderly as she

spoke.

"There I was, stuck in a loveless marriage. No excitement, no passion, no *danger* – just suffocating safeness and security. Pete was killing me with his horrific *niceness*. Outside, I could keep up appearances, be the 'happy little wife'; but inside, I was dead. Absolutely dead."

She went on quietly, as if to herself.

"Then I met Nick. That was in San Francisco, just over a year ago. It seems like yesterday. All at once, Nick awoke something in me I had never known. Passion that was all consuming; burning – it crossed the line from passion into *obsession*. Every second of every day was taken up with figuring out how to be with him again. Nothing else mattered. I had tasted life," here she looked tenderly into Nick's eyes, "I had tasted you. I *had* to have you."

She looked angrily back at her aggressors.

"I didn't care what he did for a living, or who he worked for. The government, secret service, whoever. It was all I could do to eat and sleep and make some pretence at normal life, so that no one would find us out – so we could go on meeting, secretly, as we did. I knew our future would be rocky. *But he is so incredible.* I would rather have pain from Nick than pleasure from Pete," she nearly spat out her husband's name in disgust.

Pete, crestfallen, crumpled to the ground; burying his face in his hands.

Amelia went on, relentlessly.

"And Pete was starting to get suspicious. Not back home, but once we got over here. Nick and I had arranged to meet at the restaurant that night, to exchange information – and also to plan our next rendezvous. It was child's play outwitting the police. But afterwards, Pete started saying things that worried me; that he 'saw something in my eyes' that scared him. And asking me questions; like if he were 'enough' for me; if the American I helped had been handsome. Things like that. And then, all of a sudden, Pete was always around me. It was nearly impossible for Nick and I to meet, even with him following us everywhere. Pete was acting jealous, something I hadn't counted on. Ever since I met Nick, I had been extra careful to always act like those mousy wives no man ever looks at. Those cutesy, sweet endearing little bores. In the end, I had to tell Pete some rigmarole about how 'permanence' (here she laughed again) was better than passion! I can't believe even *he* swallowed that one."

She helped slump Nick into a sitting position.

"Darling, darling," she began, earnestly. "Can you get up? Can you walk? We're getting out of here."

"Amelia," Nick said weakly. "You can't do this. I won't let you throw your life away for me."

"Nick, I *had* no life before you came. I'm not leaving here without you."

"Sadly," their antagonist interposed, "I'm afraid you're not leaving here *with* him, either. In point of fact, no one here is leaving. Not until I get what I came for."

"Nick, let's give it to him. It's our only chance."

"Amelia, you don't know who you're dealing with."

"I know I want to live, with you, forever and ever. This is our only chance for that."

Nick was silent for a moment, considering. In the interlude, Kent chided Amelia.

"I must say I am a little surprised at you, Mrs. Franklin. Surprised, and a little shocked. Saul – I'm sorry, he's 'Nick' to you, isn't he? That's an alias I hadn't heard before. In either case, Nick is really a most surprising choice. I mean *for you*. I did have you pegged completely wrong – little mousy stay at home, as you said; not worth a second look. I had no idea still waters ran so deep – or so hot. I must say, though, you're showing a surprising lack of interest in your husband – you remember him, don't you? Nice little chap here, just got his heart ripped out? – as I say, in your *husband's* fate. I had planned on killing him to force you to talk. Now I'm not so sure I wouldn't be doing you a service."

Amelia looked insolently at Kent.

"I'm a depraved woman in love. Let's leave it at that. But," she added, insistently, "If you only knew what life is like for us, day after endless day" – here her voice catched, and she took a moment before finally flinging her head back and saying, defiantly,

"Given the choice, any woman who is honest with herself would have chosen as I did."

"Yes, well – you tell yourself that at night, if it helps you sleep, my dear. Saul," here he addressed his captive, poking him with his shoe. "It seems like you've got a 'keeper' here. Can't say that I envy you, though; rather the needy type, I should say. Much like an albatross around the neck, what? In either case, looks like it's up to you, my dear man. Will you talk?"

"Never," came the quiet but firm response.

"Much as I thought. Quite right; good show, and all that. No problem. Now that I know what side her bread's buttered on, I'll just get the girl to talk. Pédro," he addressed the second youth, "Come in here and break both his arms."

"Don't you touch him!" Amelia was screaming, kicking, and scratching at her captors' eyes like a wild cat. "Don't touch him!"

"Go ahead, Pédro. I've got her."

"Nick! No!"

Just as Pedro's stick was poised to strike the bound man, a shot rang out for the second time that morning.

"*Pare!* Stop! *Isto es las policias!*"

Inspector de Sousa stood in the doorway. A dozen other officers quickly disarmed Manuel (who had been eagerly waiting for Pete to speak all this time), and overpowered the other two men. In a moment, Stevenson, now handcuffed, joined the crowd.

Amelia gently relinquished Nick to one of the officers, who tended to his bonds. She stood up, placed her hands on her hips, and faced de Sousa squarely.

"And just what took you so long?" she demanded.

The harried look leaving the man's face, de Sousa smiled broadly at Amelia, bowed ceremoniously and said,

"A thousand pardons, *Señhora.*"

CHAPTER TWELVE

It was the last day of the Franklin's vacation. Tomorrow morning, they would start their long trip home – first, a boat trip to São Miguel (a police cruiser this time; Ándre's boat was still in dry dock); then, from there, a two-hour flight west to Lisbon; then, finally, the eight hour, trans-Atlantic journey back to the East Coast.

They still had tonight, however; and tonight was for celebrating.

They had all assembled one last time – the Franklins, Inspector de Sousa and Nick Adams – for an evening meal;

that long, drawn-out collation that Europeans have perfected as an art form.

After the waiter had brought their after-dinner drinks, Nick pushed back his chair and boyishly ran his fingers through his hair.

"Alright," he said, "I've been patient long enough. I'm supposed to be the one in the intelligence racket; but you guys have me totally in the dark here. How did you find us out there, de Sousa? And, more importantly, how did you two stay alive long enough for anyone to find you? Those were some pretty tough characters you were up against, especially for civilians. You two *are* civilians, aren't you?"

Pete and Amelia laughed.

"Yes. Just two ordinary American tourists."

"Hardly 'ordinary.' Come on; somebody clue me in."

"Why don't you tell us your part, Inspector," Amelia offered, cordially.

Clearly his throat, the Inspector began formally.

"As you please, *Señhora*. First, permit me to say, *Señhor* Franklin, that I have the most regard for your wife. She is most brave, and most imaginative woman. I think most highly the thoughts of her. However, this was not always the case. In fact, in beginning, we dislike one another right away. Is true. She pull the sheep's skin over my eyes when we first met; after that, it becomes like a game for her. Lucky for all, she decide to trust me and stop playing her game before the end came."

"One thing I don't understand," interjected Pete, "Was why you were trying to arrest Nick in the first place. I mean, at O Birraca, when Amelia helped him escape. I hate to be simplistic, but isn't he one of 'the good guys?'"

Nick's merry laugh rang out.

"You can call me that if you like. It'd be the first time, and I kind of like it. Yes, de Sousa certainly gave me a run for my money." He went on, "Naturally, I can't tell you too much about my part in all this – this case is technically still open and a lot of the information involved is classified. I can tell you that I work for our government's intelligence community. Stevenson and the man you knew as Kent have been under surveillance for some time and I was sent out here to check up on their activities. It was all supposed to be cut-and-dried kind of work. But it was more like stumbling onto a wasp's net. And we had underestimated both the scope of their racket, and how well organized and how high up their disinformation network was. Within a day of my arriving here, I found my name on the Interpol wanted list – for murder, no less."

Nick smiled. "That wouldn't have been so bad. But my emergency contact out here – the real Matthew Kent – had been called back to the US for a family emergency. So I had both the police and the other guys looking for me; I could never be sure who was pursuing me; or whether I'd be arrested or shot when they finally caught up to me. When I broke into that basement window, I was pretty hard up; without a friend in the world," here he turned appreciatively towards Amelia, "Till I met you."

Amelia smiled. "Glad I could be of help, Nick. But, we're interrupting the inspector."

"*Muito obrigada, Señhora.*" The inspector resumed, stiffly, "As I was saying, early on I have the suspicions about *Señhora* Franklin, here. When we get *Señhor* Adams' fingerprints off the window, I know she is lying about not to see him. So, I ask myself, *why*? The explanation most simple is that she is, *come se dice*, in 'cahoots' with the man, a man wanted for murder. So I confront her next day at her villa. Tell her I have discovered her lie. I ask for the truth, and even offer her protection. She refuse me, absolutely. But something – maybe the way she hold her head; or the way she raise the eyebrows; even the way she is trying not to smile – all these things tell me, 'She is playing the game with you, de Sousa.'"

Here he turned to Amelia.

"I have been an officer for many years, *Señhora*. Often I see the guilty man lie. Sometimes I see the innocent man panic, and tell the false stories that make him look guilty. But never have I known someone to lie to me, to obstruct the justice, *just for the thrill of it*. That is what you were doing, am I not correct, *Señhora*?"

"It's rather embarrassing to admit it now, but yes, that's pretty much it. In my defense, I can honestly say that I didn't really like you at the time (I think you're an absolute dear, now); and I did have some vague feelings of patriotism – you know, protecting a fellow American, and all that. By the way," here she addressed Nick, "Now that you don't need me to keep your confounded gum wrapper safe, I guess you'll be wanting it back."

She tugged at the hair tie, and her dark hair cascaded around her face.

"Guess you won't be letting me in on what it was – no? I was afraid of that."

Sighing, she turned back to de Sousa. "Anyway, where was I? Oh, yes. Well, I guess deep down, Inspector, what I loved was just the challenge, the 'thrill' if you will, of finally being involved in a mysterious adventure, instead of always just reading about one. It was like getting the leading role in an exciting drama; I – I didn't want to give that up."

"You are a woman of the honesty most exceptional, *Señhora*. Yes, after our meeting, I see she is no criminal, just a woman having the fun. But she no realize the rules of the game she play. So I give her the warnings; tell her husband to stay by her side. And when we rise to leave, I make the pretence of using the phone to get her alone for a small moment. In those few seconds I tell her I know what she is; that she just plays for the fun. But I assure her, but certainly she will be killed if she continue to, *come se dice*, flirt with the danger. 'Dead by week's end,' is the expression I use, *não es verdadeiro, Señhora?*"

"Yes. And very convincing it was, too. Although, at the time, I never would have admitted it."

"Yes, you take my assistance then, but not gladly."

"I don't understand what you're talking about," said Nick. "What could he give you in just a few seconds that would be so important?"

"*Señhor* de Sousa very graciously gave a fool a *chance*. But we'll get to that in a moment. What I'd like to know now is when you stopped suspecting Nick to be a murderer, and started getting suspicious of Kent. He seemed genuine enough."

"Ah, that. As to *Señhor* Adams, I have to admit I figure that out just by luck. I have a little weakness," he confessed in a low voice. "I love the e-mail. The internet. Yes, do not look so startled. We are not so backwards a country as you think. I go on internet, ten, twenty times a day – sometimes, " here he shook his head ashamedly, "When I should be working. To make me feel not so guilty, I also check some sites for my work – and Interpol is one of them. When I see *Señhor* Adams' name suddenly appear, I am surprised; and not only because he is supposed to be in my area. Every listing in IPOL is dated; it show how long it has been posted on the internet – and Adams' say it has been posted for two weeks.

But I check IPOL once a day, maybe more. *Señhor* Adams' picture only appeared *that day*; I would have noticed it if it had been there before. So immediately I have the suspicions. Who is this *Señhor* Adams; and, of the most importance, who is tampering with IPOL to make him seem like the criminal?"

"As to Kent, it was something you told me that made me suspect. You told me the Vice Consul *himself* had told you I could not detain you here without the reason. But I knew the Vice Consul had gone back to America for his mother's funeral – our office actually send flowers for the occasion. So I know you speak to someone pretending to be other than he is; most likely a dangerous man. Besides Adams, I had received reports of other criminals in Fíal – Stevenson, and another whose name was not listed; only a photograph. With these men already here, that is when I insist there is no more time to waste; that *Señhora must* take my help, or it will be too late."

"But – you'll excuse me if I'm being dense here – let's go back to my last question. What help, exactly, did you give her," demanded Nick, "Other than your good advice, of course," he added respectfully.

"Help came in a little paper bag," Amelia said in answer, chuckling, "But I'm getting a little ahead of myself. It's true that I was having fun with de Sousa in the beginning. I was enjoying immensely the part I was playing. I was confident that Nick posed no threat to us (call it woman's intuition); so that just left me with an Inspector to toy with. It was wicked, I know; but since I wasn't doing anything technically illegal, I figured he wasn't much of a threat to me, either. But when de Sousa finally rammed home the fact that there really were other players involved, players that could and would harm Pete and myself – and even *our children* – well that's when I stopped being a silly girl on her second honeymoon and started being an adult again. I had had my fun, but at what cost? I admitted as much to de Sousa, and he offered me an out; as I said, in the form of a little paper bag. I didn't know what was in it at the time – he gave it to me in the hall when Pete was out getting the car and I stuffed it in my handbag; I remember I had a hard time making it fit. But when I opened it later at the hotel, after our villa had been ransacked, Pete and I had a long talk about it and made our plan."

She turned, smiling, to Pete.

"You know," she said to the rest of the group, "Pete really was fantastic about the whole thing. I mean, he's always great; but more so than usual. What I mean is, we had just been having an argument about some foolishness or other; married people do, you know. Nothing serious, of course; one doesn't stay married for ten years without really loving and understanding one another. But one does get so silly at times, what with too much time on one's hands and nothing else to worry about. What I mean is, we were practically not even on speaking terms at the time – and then, I tell him all about de

Sousa, and his plan, and our involvement and possible danger – and he rises to the occasion like a champ. And I think he had the hardest part of all to play, because he had to pretend to be so *dumb*. And he really is quite clever, you know."

Nick looked about to burst. "The paper bag?" he nearly exploded.

"Okay," Amelia laughed, "I'm getting to it. Back at the hotel, we stayed up all night, making up our minds. Pete was all for getting out right away, and I agreed (that's how we got involved in that Ándre fiasco). But I also wanted a contingency plan, in case – for whatever reason – we were unable to leave the island. In all the thrillers I've ever read (and I've read nearly all our local library has to offer) people land in trouble because they never conceive of the worst actually happening; they're always so shocked when it does. We turned that on its head and said, 'what's the worst possible outcome'? De Sousa had alluded to our children being threatened somehow; so we got on the phone and woke up Pete's brother – he's a cop back home – we just said there was some problem over here and asked him to take our kids upstate with him and his wife to their cabin for a while. Just told him it was important. Alan was great about it; no questions asked. So that took care of that."

Amelia continued.

"The next thing we could think of, was one or both of us being kidnapped (you see we were one the right track here!), and one of us being tortured as a way to get the other to talk. This was a pretty unpleasant idea, and a little harder to make a contingency plan for. I mean, neither one of us has an incredibly high pain tolerance threshold; and I think I would break down immediately if anyone so much as broke one of Pete's fingernails. So we came up with the idea that we would *pretend* not to care what happened to each other, so that they couldn't use us as pawns against each other. This seemed a little weak; so we added in the idea that I was madly in love with Nick and would do anything for him. Pete (very foolishly) had actually been getting a little jealous of the 'desperate American' figure anyway, so this seemed the natural way to go. All this would hopefully take the focus off of us (which was our main objective at the time) and direct it to Nick. Sorry about that," she added, sheepishly.

"Hey, it goes with the territory," Nick replied, nonchalantly.

"And, I still had that cryptic message of yours to try out, if the need arose. So we thought we had our bases covered enough to try to get off the island ourselves, and had half-decided not to use Sousa's help after all, when we ran into him in the hotel lobby."

"I am perpetually thankful that you did, *Señhora*."

"So am I, Inspector. I can't believe I was actually going to walk out that door, away from all help, or police protection – well, your last warning convinced me. I decided to finally take your advice, once and for all; to place myself in your hands. You know, I place a lot of stock in woman's intuition. I disliked you, so I kept waiting for my intuition to dislike you, too. But, luckily, it didn't cooperate. Nick I had never been afraid of. Kent made my slightly suspicious. But you, Inspector, despite my best efforts, got a passing grade."

She looked mischievously at Nick.

"Okay. Here's how I did it. I was still carrying around de Sousa's little bag with me, undecided if I would ever need it. After my mind was finally made up, I pretended to trip and sprain my ankle going down the lobby steps. My ankles are infamously bad, so it was no problem acting the part. While I was supposed to be wrapping my ankle, I got Pete to hold back the well-wishers long enough for me to open the bag undetected. Inside was the hypodermic needle we had looked at the night before; a syringe filled with clear fluid, in which was floating a tiny particle (about the size of a grain of rice). The enclosed instructions described the particle as a type of injectible microchip. I had heard of such things being used in wild animals to track their migration; or as a way to find lost house pets. I wasn't thrilled about using myself as a literal guinea pig; but Pete and I had decided that if something did happen to us, we wanted the police to have at least a chance at finding us. That is the 'chance' I mentioned before.

She sighed and went on briskly.

"So I injected it, in the soft tissue just below my calf and above of my Achilles tendon. I didn't really know what I was doing, so it left a mark; but I got it in, in the end. I wrapped up my ankle as usual; it just covered the spot. I hobbled out of the hotel hoping I had made the right choice."

"You sure did!" Nick said, emphatically. "If you hadn't made that decision, not only would the police never have found you; I would have been a gonner. They picked me up right after São Fortunato's, you know. They were only keeping me alive long enough for 'Kent' to kill me; I had interfered with some of his business in the past, and he wanted to pay me back, personally. You really have turned out to be my guardian angel, Mrs. Franklin."

"Please; after the spectacle I made of myself the other day, I would hope you would at least call me Amelia."

Nick blushed. "Uh, yes. Amelia," he said, uncomfortably.

"As I was saying," Amelia continued, her eyes twinkling. "We tried getting off the island, but Ándre put an end to all that. Him and his crazy boat." She shook her head, reminiscently. "They nabbed us later that night, you know; and Pete got pretty beat up. The whole trip to Píco, I kept wondering if we could carry out our plan. On the one hand, I was feeling wide-awake, fully alive and ready for adventure. But on the other, I was already so viscerally shaken-up by seeing Pete hurt just a *little* bit, I wasn't at all sure I could be 'blasé' as we had planned if something worse happened to him."

She went on.

"Well, I won't go over all the details. That guy Stevenson wanted us to 'talk.' From watching old movies, I knew it was useless to keep insisting we didn't know anything (even though, in this case, we really didn't!); it always just seems to antagonize the bad guys. So, I let him believe I was 'in the know,' and Pete played up beautifully as the deceived husband. It was tricky, because we were just playing by the seat of our collective pants, so to speak; but we read each other perfectly, I thought."

"Honey, you were the great actress," Pete said, smiling at her. "I was just following your lead."

"Not all the time. Remember, *you* took the initiative to steal that cell phone. That was pretty daring."

"And," Pete remarked, ruefully, "It would have been even better if I had trusted de Sousa and called the police, instead of calling the ring-leader of the whole gang!"

"We couldn't foresee that one, dear. Or maybe *I* could have, if I had only fully trusted my intuition! You know, for as nice as he was when we met him, there was something that kept me from trusting Kent completely; but, at the time, I chalked that up to growing paranoia on my part. I told myself not everyone could be 'in on it,' and tried to force myself to trust the guy. It figures; the one time my intuition really gives me a warning, and I ignore it!"

She continued.

"Anyway, I had been expecting de Sousa to come storming

in at any moment and save us. I mean, I had the chip in; he should be able to pick up the signal and come to our rescue and capture the criminals; I couldn't imagine what was taking so long."

"Again, the many apologies, *Señhora*," de Sousa interposed. "I was myself in the agony not being able to trace you, once you had finally put the trust in me. I would never have given myself the forgiveness if something happen to you. I had no counted on the interference this isolated part of the island presents. It was something most unusual."

"Yes," Pete agreed, "I remember I had trouble getting a signal for the cell call I made."

"Hmm. Well, I did my best trying to stay alive, solely for *your* sake, de Sousa," Amelia went on, ingratiatingly. "But when I finally played my last card (that mumbo-jumbo about the 'data,' and having to meet Saul, and all that) and it didn't help us, I knew I had to do something to buy us more time. I had to find a way to stall those guys. And, then it came to me."

Here she looked apologetically at Nick.

"I hope you understand, I never meant to put you in even greater danger. But, I was in a tight spot; I was so afraid they would hurt Pete, I had forgotten about being afraid for myself or anyone else. I figured they were planning on killing you, anyway (that does sound callous, doesn't it!), so if I could get their attention away from Pete and fix it on you – well, it wasn't a very well thought-out plan, I admit; but I was desperately looking for any way to buy even a few minutes for de Sousa to get there. And I guess I kind of justified it by thinking that, if I did give the police enough time to arrive, they would save you, too; which they did. So, you – you do understand, don't you, Nick?"

"Madame," Nick said graciously, smiling and making a little mock bow that would have looked more natural coming from the inspector, "I am forever indebted to you for saving my life – twice over. Far be it from me to criticize your personal motivations, whatever they may have been."

Amelia smiled. "Thank you, Nick; you're sweet. So," she went on, " I deliberately put you in harm's way when I flung myself at you and started using the plot of every novel I'd ever read against you. I hadn't really decided what to say yet, or how to play out my part; I was still mentally sifting through the dozens of characters I keep stored up in my head. But once I decided upon the role of aggrieved housewife, finding passion and meaning in life with a younger man – the rest was (I hate to admit it) kind of easy; and as close as you can get to 'fun' when you're also that close to death."

"You were amazing," Nick said. "I was only just conscious, you know; coming off of a rough session with one of those kids. I remember responding (like an ass, I'm sure), that I 'wouldn't let you do it' and 'what about Pete?' and all the rest of it. But I said those things, not to add credibility to your performance, but honestly, because I couldn't tell that it *was* a performance in the first place."

There was a momentary pause.

"I'm glad I was so convincing, for all our sakes," Amelia responded quietly. She went on quickly; "When de Sousa finally came busting in, I remember having thought just a second before, 'I'm running out of material here. What in the world am I going to say next? They're going to catch on to me.' I'm glad you didn't let us down, Inspector."

"As am I, *Señhora*," he responded, gravely.

"And Pete was fantastic," Amelia continued. "Actually crumpling to the ground, and heaving those great sighs, and all the rest. You were very convincing."

"I had to cover my face with my hands," Pete responded, good-natured as always. "I didn't trust myself. First, I found myself smiling; then, I actually had to stifle a few laughs when you really got going there."

"Peter," Amelia scolded, trying not to smile. "And I had hoped you'd be just the tiniest bit jealous!"

"Don't worry; I've learned my lesson not to take you for granted, dear. In fact, I think I just might get jealous of you more often in the future."

"Oh, I'm so glad," Amelia responded gleefully, clapping her hands together like a delighted child. "I'm so glad!"

"You are a couple certainly of the most unusual," de Sousa commented, as he drained his glass.

* * *

The Franklins stood on the tarmac landing strip. The small, propeller plane parked in front of them was still being packed with parcels – mostly hothouse pineapples for the mainland - but the airport personnel made some concession for luggage as well.

Pete and Nick Adams had just shaken hands.

"Thank you again, Pete, for all you did to help me," Nick said.

"You have Amelia to thank for that one. I did pretty much everything I could *not* to help you; but that was before I knew you were a decent guy. Anyway, good luck out here."

"Yes, I still have some loose ends to tie-up; tracking down all the small fry of the organization and whatnot. But, thanks to you, the police got Stevenson and Montaigne (that's Kent, to you guys); and they were the top dogs, at least for this branch. My work goes on and on, really."

"Until justice and righteousness is restored in the universe?" Pete queried, smiling.

"Something like that. Well, good-bye, again."

Then, looking down and idly kicking some crumbled asphalt with the tip of his shoe, he began, reddening,

"I know I have no right to ask. It's what those English guys would call 'awful cheek' on my part. But, *could* I have a few words with Amelia?"

The word 'alone' stood unspoken between them.

"Certainly," Pete replied, smiling, "She'd enjoy that."

"Peter!"

Pete tossed his linen jacket over one shoulder, and jauntily walked towards the mobile stair, which had been nosed up to the body of the plane. He ascended it, and disappeared inside.

The hot sun poured down on the lone couple from above, and radiated up from the black airstrip. Their cheeks flushed, and tiny pricks of moisture ran down the backs of their necks.

"So, this is goodbye," Nick began.

"Yes, goodbye, Mr. Adams," Amelia held out her hand and Nick took it. "I hope you'll be safe, what with me going, and all."

"So do I."

There was an awkward pause, during which Nick did not relinquish her hand.

"You know, you're an incredible woman," Nick ventured, again.

"Thank you. I'm sure you're a very wonderful man, as well," Amelia responded, politely.

"And that's it?"

"What's 'it'?"

"I mean, you get on that plane; and I go back to work; and we never see each other again?"

"I think you know that's what will happen," she answered, gently.

Nick looked away, scowling. "But the things you said to me

– I know you say now that you never meant them. That they were just a way to stay alive."

Here he took both her hands in his, and went on earnestly.

"But I was there. I heard your voice. My God, Amelia, when I woke up and saw you there in that hole, coming to me like an angel – holding me in your arms - saying those words – I believed in them; I believed in *you*. I thought to myself, 'I am the luckiest man in the world. We *will* get out of here alive, and be together,' just as you said. Amelia," his voice cracked as he leaned towards her, and whispered, passionately, "Look in my eyes and tell me I mean nothing to you."

Amelia's gaze never fell. She said, in a very quiet voice,

"I can't say that, Nick. You don't mean 'nothing' to me. You are handsome and brave; and I have loved every exciting moment we've shared together, and I will never be able to forget you. But, Pete and I have been through a lot; and a lot more than what you and I have experienced. Not just thrills and excitement; but boredom, and mortgage payments, and taking care of each other when we caught the flu, and a thousand and one silly little things that you wouldn't think bond people together – but they do. And not just little things, either, Nick. Pete and I have had our babies together; and I think, after that happens, at least for me, it would be nearly impossible to break that tie."

Nick looked disappointed; but, as he sighed, Amelia could feel his physical tension begin to wane. She went on, encouragingly,

"Anyway, Nick, infidelity is overrated. And you don't really know me, and I don't really know you from, from -"

"Adam?"

"Good! You see? You're getting your sense of humor back; you're recovering already."

She went on.

"It's simple, really. Some girls *can* kindle passion in men, and keep that fire going. They have torrid affairs, and drive every man they meet crazy without even trying to. I know who I am, and I *can't* do all those things. Some women are like hot-crossed buns; I'm more like honey-wheat bread – sweet and wholesome. It's a little disappointing, but there it is. There was a time when I wished I could be more captivating; to possess that gift or curse, or whatever you want to call it. But I don't, and that's that; and it's all for the best I'm sure. I mean, some of my best friends over the years have been men, men I was not romantic with at all. If I had been an absolute siren, I would have missed out on all of that; and it would have been a tragic loss. I think most women waste most of their time wishing to be something they're not. I don't anymore. I know who I am. I'm *me*."

The twin propellers spun slowly, then sputtered noisily into action. The cargo hatch was closed with a bang, and a flight attendant at the head of the stairs motioned to Amelia.

"Goodbye, Nick. Be safe," Amelia had to nearly shout to be

heard over the engines.

He made no immediate response. Then, as if making up his mind, his smile spread slowly as he said,

"You're wrong, you know."

"What?" Amelia yelled.

"You're wrong," Nick repeated in a louder voice. "About not being captivating. You have it; you just choose to hide it."

Leaning forward, he kissed her on the cheek.

"Goodbye, Amelia."

And with that, she turned and hurried toward the stairs.

EPILOGUE

"*Q*uiera um bebida? Would you like a drink?" the weary flight attendant asked.
"No, thanks."

The stewardess ambled down the aisle.

Pete and Amelia sat together in the small, noisy aircraft and peered out of their tiny window. There had been no land visible for over an hour, now. Below them, glittering with the sun's reflection, was the enormous, blue expanse. Tiny specks of white (which must in reality have been colossal breakers) showed them that they were beginning their slow descent to the mainland. From time to time, tiny wisps of cloud scuttled past their view. Amelia felt her ears pop with the change in cabin pressure.

Then, all at once, they saw it.

Amelia had remembered it from her first visit ten years ago; she had missed it upon re-entering the country three weeks previous, due to the weather.

Now, there it was.

Jutting out of the ocean, almost like a fairy-tale landscape, was the coast of Portugal. Enormous purple cliffs appeared suddenly, like stately giants keeping watch over their realm. They seemed at once powerful and serene; like mighty explorers of old, looking out towards the New World. Amelia saw those cliffs again, and smiled in recognition, as if at long lost friends.

"Pete, isn't it beautiful."

"Yes, dear."

She didn't notice he was looking at her.

"Let's go away again," Amelia said breathlessly, turning in her seat to face Pete. "For our fifteenth and twentieth and twenty-fifth, for all the anniversaries we can afford to go. There's so much to see, and so many places to go; so many adventures to have yet - *together*."

For a second, Pete had an overwhelming desire to never go away again in his life. To stay home, with Amelia and the kids. To stay where things were safe and predictable and where you knew where you stood. To live in a place where danger and fear and uncertainty were far away.

But then he looked again at his wife.

Her eyes were shining expectantly. She looked so happy and funny and young; and Pete realized all at once that she was looking that way *because she was looking at him* and seeing their life together laid out before them.

At last, confronting his own worst fear, and finally realizing that he was indeed 'enough' for Amelia, Pete Franklin patted his wife's hand and said, endearingly,

"Whatever you'd like, dear. Whatever you'd like."

ABOUT THE AUTHOR

Teresa Manidis wrote her debut novel, *Moon of Honey - Lua de Mel*, over a three-week period. The book you have just read (with very few exceptions) is identical to that first manuscript.

"Writing this book was one of the most exciting things I've ever done. It came to me so fast, I could barely keep up," she says of the experience. "When I would sit down to write, I could clearly see, say, chapter two, and the *tiniest* bit of chapter three. It was all moving so fast, I felt I had to write down what I saw on a daily basis, in case tomorrow brought chapters three and four and chapter two would be lost to me forever."

Manidis never thought writing a novel would be like this. "When I say I 'watched my book unfold' it sounds ridiculous, but really that's how it was for me. I was more or less just writing down what I saw. Amelia *had* brown hair. Kent *wore* those silly cargo shorts and flip-flops. The roof of the abandoned dairy *was* made out of green corrugated plastic – I couldn't change anything, even if I tried. One example comes halfway through chapter three. For the plot to run smoothly, I needed the Franklins to have a spirited argument, make up, and be totally reconciled by the end of the chapter. So I began writing the dialogue for a 'friendly' argument. But, try as I might to reel them in, the couple just kept getting angrier and angrier. Tempers flared. Words were exchanged. By the time Amelia slammed the door in Pete's face, I gave up and had to rework the rest of the book from there," Manidis recounts, laughingly. "The two of them together were too much for me."

Manidis attended DeSales University and majored in English, where she wrote for the university newspaper and won several small writing contests as an undergraduate. But it was not until her senior year that her writing skills were officially recognized, when she was awarded the Ross Baker Memorial Award - her university's highest honor for excellence in writing. "I had several excellent writing instructors," she recalls, "Who took me from a more Dickens-like style (wordy, verbose) all the way across the spectrum to something more like Hemingway (more sparse, and journalistic)."

But Manidis' writing career began long before college. "I began writing my first novel when I was nine years old. I remember watching TV one day with my Dad (a *much* better writer than I will ever be). He was disgusted with the plot of the show, and said, 'Teresa, you could write something better than that.' Taking him at his word, I marched downstairs and began typing away on what was then a state-of-the-art computer (I distinctly remember how the words looked on that old, plasma screen – a dark brown field with bright orange text). My book was called *Five* and chronicled the struggles of five Mexican bank robbers. I made it all the way to chapter three before my fourth grade geography caught up with me – I couldn't remember if Mexico City was surrounded by desert, jungle or tundra. I eventually gave up on that novel, but the belief that I could write stayed with me, thanks to Dad's prompting. I dedicate this, my first *completed* novel, to him."

Moon of Honey is based on some real life experiences Manidis shared with her husband, John. "We traveled to the Azore Islands for our honeymoon. Many parts of *Lua de Mel* – the scenery, hotels, churches, restaurants, even the menus Amelia and Pete enjoy on their trip – all spring from real life. Although we were never involved in political intrigue, the excitement of two Americans exploring a beautiful and exotic locale was very real for us."

Manidis is very fond of her hero and heroine. "Simply put, Pete and Amelia *are* us. When I am a better writer, I will be able to make my main character male, fat, balding and 65. Until then, when I write, my heroine is loosely based on me – or what I'd like to be. And the character of Pete – easy going, patient and true - is very like my husband."

When asked if she is bothered that her action-packed book has been referred to as "Nancy Drew for Grown-Ups,"

Manidis smiles broadly. "What's wrong with that?" she asks. "In fact, what a compliment! When you think that Nancy Drew is one of best-known and most beloved fictional characters of all time. Just because an inordinate number of adventures come her way, we can't begrudge her that; we read to escape to a more (not less) interesting world than our own."

When asked if there were other great fictional couples that she admires, she was quick to respond. "Tommy and Tuppence. Agatha Christie's brilliant, 'plucky' married sleuths. Those novels are masterpieces – not just for their masterfully thought-out plots, but also for their light-heartedness and fun, something very difficult to weave into a murder or spy mystery. I love Tommy and Tuppence – everyone does. For all their faults (and maybe because of them) you could always tell they were crazy in love with each other. That fact, along with the feeling that they were enjoying themselves – always just about to break out laughing – make us care for them, and make their dangerous escapades all the more thrilling and enjoyable to read."

Manidis lives in Pennsylvania with her husband and four children. When not writing, she enjoys spending time with her family, swimming and traveling.

She had this to say in closing. "I had stopped writing for a number of years after college, and when asked why I said having something to write is kind of like being pregnant. Either you have something wonderful, deep inside of you – or you don't. There was nothing for years and years; and then when this finally 'happened,' the novel almost wrote itself. I am not so naïve as to think it will always be this easy and enjoyable; but this one was and it was great."

" It was a lot of fun to write this book, and I think that shows through in its quick-pace and light-heartedness. I have four books 'in queue' in my head at all times (not the most comfortable thing!) and these, although as yet unwritten, are 'finished' in the sense that I can already 'see' them clearly, all the way to their completion. Now that *Lua de Mel* is published, I can't wait to start putting these down on paper. In fact, I think I'll go do that right now."